M000031178

The *Marquess* and the *Midwife*

A Christmas Novella

ALINA K. FIELD

To Sorry,

Happy reading!

Mary

DEDICATION

For Albert and Alicia

Finding the woman he lost turned out to be easy.
Winning her is another matter.

Once upon a time, the younger brother of a marquess fell in love with his sister's companion. He was sent off to war, and she was just sent off, and they both landed in very different worlds.

Now Virgil Radcliffe has returned from his self-imposed exile on the Continent to take up his late brother's title and discover the whereabouts of the only woman he's ever loved.

Abandoned by her lover and dismissed by her employer, Ameline Dawes has found a respectable identity as a Waterloo widow, a new life as a midwife, and a safe, secure home for her twin girls. Called to London at Christmas to attend her benefactress's lying-in, she finds herself confronted by an unexpected house guest--a man determined to woo her anew and win her again.

But, is loving the new Marquess of Wallingford a mistake Ameline cannot afford to repeat?

CHAPTER ONE

IN THE GREAT SPRAWL OF LONDON, WHERE would he find her?

Virgil Radcliffe, Marquess of Wallenford, pushed open the coach door himself and swung out on his good leg.

Hackwell House rose before him, all gleaming windows and freshly painted trim. Last year Steven Beauverde, the latest Earl of Hackwell, had uncovered his own brother's killer. Surely he could help discover a woman gone missing in London.

If she were here. If she still lived.

As the coach wobbled around a corner, Ameline Dawes braced her heels and locked each child to her. "Very soon, girls," she said, infusing her voice with loud cheer.

"Move out of the bloody—"

At the curse from outside she covered their small ears and pulled both little heads tight against her.

"And you'll see Thomas and Robby again," she cried, hoping to drown the coachman's shouted rebuke at whoever had cursed him.

It wouldn't do for those words to fly out in an earl's nursery.

Outside, the streets were just as dank and dreary and dirty as she remembered from her confinement here three years before. London in late December was no place for a lady to bring a babe into the world, and no place for a lady—well, a former gentlewoman—to bring the two squirming souls Ameline had tucked on each side of her, her bright, beautiful girls.

She squeezed her eyes and took a deep breath—fatherless they were, but still the lights of her life.

She'd rather have spent Christmas at their cottage in the grounds of the children's home at Longview, where she worked as a teacher and general healer to the children served by Lady Hackwell's charity, and midwife to the local women. Still, the journey had been uneventful, if one could discount twin tantrums, a bout of motion sickness, and assorted disputes over best access to the windows.

She did discount them, as best as her patience would allow. Between the girls' antics and the muddy winter roads, she was fair wrung out. Well, in truth, she was fair wrung out most days, so why should this one be different?

And from the contents of Lord Hackwell's last express, she could plan on a full night ahead and more stuffed-down worry.

She glanced at her twins and couldn't help smiling. She was rightfully proud that she'd been able to provide for them, and grateful for her benefactress. The trials of the journey were small compared to what Lady Hackwell had done for her. And in spite of her impending confinement, Lady Hackwell had promised a celebration of the girls' Christmas birthday.

Because of her confinement, Ameline could be certain any guest list would be limited to the one old army friend of his lordship who Lady Hackwell had said would be visiting. There'd be no chance she'd run into someone from her past life, before she'd become Mrs. Dawes, teacher and midwife.

"I'm hungry." Dee said in the throaty voice that made people mistake her for a boy.

"Me too." Em echoed her larger twin.

"Soon, little ones."

Outside, crowds bunched and mingled at the edge of the traffic, all that humanity crowded together so a woman could barely breathe. London had never been her favorite destination. And London in a dismal December, the days so short one had scarcely five hours of grey daylight, and so abominably moist one could barely feel any warmth and—

"Look." Dee pressed her nose to the window.

Ameline peeled back her dark mood and forced a smile, reminding herself that London was also a place that could be filled with wonders, especially in the week before Christmas. They'd passed shop windows hung with pine boughs and red ribbons, seen girls hawking tied bundles of mistletoe, and outside, here on the edge of the park, was a swarthy street peddler turning the crank on a hand organ while his uniformed monkey danced.

"That is a monkey," Ameline said. "Like the picture in the book at home."

"Mukkey." Dee bounced against the padded leather of Lord Hackwell's traveling chaise, tossing off the rug that had warmed them, sending Em into a howl.

Ameline rescued the blanket from the floor. As her head came up, the chaise turned a corner into a square lined with massive townhouses.

She settled both girls and tucked the warm wool back around them.

"I want to see," Em moaned.

"Go back," Dee said.

Ameline took in a breath. What with tending to Lady Hackwell and assisting her teacher, Mrs. Crawford, with a birth expected to be difficult, there would be little time for looking at shop windows and monkeys. No time actually. "He was a frightfully funny sight, wasn't he?" They'd turned into Berkeley Square where, *please God*, they'd soon find worthier distractions.

Dee squawked and Em started up with her, the way cats did when a fight was underway.

"Look, Dulciana, Emma. We've stopped."

They had indeed. The door opened and a young man in livery set down the coach stairs. A dark patch covered one of his eyes and part of the scar that ran from his forehead to his jaw.

In the three-and-a-half years since Waterloo, England had been filled with displaced and often permanently maimed soldiers, some who'd served under the earl when he'd been mere Major Beauverde. This was another of Lord Hackwell's veterans, the sharp livery making him look as if he'd rejoined his regiment.

The earl and his lady were ones to take in wounded strays, and didn't Ameline know it.

The footman handed her out and the scents of the city rushed into her lungs—coal smoke and damp, and a flavor one didn't want to think too much about. Why Lady Hackwell had chosen to have her baby in London, instead of her country estate, she couldn't fathom.

Dee and Em jostled each other at the coach door, but both pink mouths opened at the sight of the young man's mangled face. He grinned and whisked them up into strong arms. "There now, little misses, we have a few muddy steps to walk, so I'll just carry you, shall I?"

Dee frowned and put a finger into the deep scar.

Ameline pulled out her instrument bag and followed the footman past two noble townhouses, to the gleaming door of Hackwell House. Another coach had blocked the way of their chaise, and servants unloaded baggage from it.

The hair on her neck fluttered. The coach was black with a burgundy trim, large and comfortable...

No. It could not be his. There were many such coaches about. This one, as grimy as it was, might even be hired.

The coach must belong to the friend Lady Hackwell had written about, the army friend who'd returned from roaming the Continent and begged a room with them. He'd be no bother to the ladies, she'd said.

The guest wouldn't be *him*. *He'd* never mentioned Lord Hackwell's name, and besides, *he* had his own grand house in town.

Strange that a man would visit during his hostess's lying in, and stranger still that the Hackwells would allow it. He must be a very good friend, indeed. And perhaps he might keep his lordship distracted during the worst of the labor.

In any case, it was none of Ameline's affair. She was no more than a special kind of servant in this business.

As she drew nearer the visitor's coach, she could see the gold tip of a heraldic shield, the rest of the insignia lurking under a coat of road grime.

Her heart thundered, and inside her gloves, her hands heated and chilled. The crosses and poppies of the Wallenford arms had been burned into her memory, but surely they were not hidden there. And surely, this coach was too tired and beaten up to be that special, grand, and very comfortable coach commissioned by the last marquess.

Tears welled and she blinked them back.

Don't be a ninny. It wasn't him. The last mention of him had been a news item that'd put him in Vienna doing some fusty task for the Crown, a task entirely inappropriate to his character. And good riddance.

And she had her own work to do. Her heart quaked and she took a deep breath to settle it. She'd been in attendance with expert midwives at many births, but this was only the third she would manage, on her own, since Mrs. Crawford was down with her back. And the other new mothers had been farmers' wives.

But...this was London, and if needs must, Lady Hackwell could call on one of Mrs. Crawford's other apprentices as well as the best accoucheur. Ameline could have the coachman return in an hour with fresh horses and be on her way home with the girls.

Yes. That would be better entirely. Her ladyship would be in good hands, and Ameline could dodge this guest of the Hackwells, whoever he might be.

Heart clanging again, she stopped short and lifted her hand to hail her chaise, only to spot it pulling away. Another servant carrying her and the girls' baggage all but plowed into her.

"Mrs. Dawes." A young maid rushed down the steps and tugged Em from the scarred footman's arms.

"Jenny." Squealing, Em crushed herself against the maid, while Dee wriggled in the footman's arms.

Ameline greeted the maid, a Longview girl who'd gone into service, and under the impassive gaze of the starched butler, Alton, they slipped in and handed over their cloaks.

Her breath eased. No handsome noblemen lurked in the hall, only servants, but a staircase loomed, shadowed at the top, daring her to risk the journey to her ladyship's room.

"The pains are started, and her ladyship keeps asking after you," Jenny said. "I'll take these two. Thomas and Robby are waiting for 'em."

Thomas and Robby were Lord Hackwell's young brother and nephew, respectively, both hellions.

Ameline hesitated.

Jenny grinned. "Don't worry. I'll keep the peace in the nursery, and the kitchen maid is there too. Mary's with Lady H."

Mary, Lady Hackwell's longtime maid-of-all-work, now ran the nursery and could easily handle four boisterous children. But her steady hand in the birthing room would be a blessing.

"Don't let them run about. They must stay in the nursery, out of the way of his lordship and his guest."

"Yes, mum, and a great lord is 'e, this guest. 'E's just arrived." Jenny took both girls by the hand. "And ever so 'andsome," she whispered with a cheeky grin. "Now let's go 'ave a biscuit before Master Thomas eats 'em all."

Ameline watched them head up the stairs, swallowing her own smile. She had tried very hard, but there'd always be a touch of the Seven Dials in Jenny.

And perhaps the world was better for that.

A masculine throat cleared. "May I carry your smaller bag, Mrs. Dawes?"

The white haired butler already held her large traveling case in one hand. The scarred footman had disappeared with the children's things. "I'll carry this one," she said. "Lead the way to her ladyship."

"Would you not like to freshen up first?"

She checked the hem of her skirt. She'd mostly kept it out of the mud, but Mrs. Crawford said cleanliness must always be the first medicine applied. She had a fresh work dress in her bag, and it would be good to be able to wash.

"Yes, thank you, and I will be but a moment."

"We are a bit short-staffed, but I can send up a kitchen maid to help—"

"No." She'd long ago abandoned dresses that required a maid. "Best to put her to heating water."

"Very well." He led her up the richly carpeted stairs. "Your chamber is just this way."

An Aubusson runner stretched from one closed door at the far left of the stairs to an opposing one at the other end. As she turned to follow Alton, she heard the click of a door latch and glanced over her shoulder. A man was exiting the far room, his form and face lost in the shadows. She turned quickly and entered her chamber.

Virgil struggled into a clean shirt and coat by himself. He'd left his own man in Dover, waiting for the rest of his crates and dealing with the infernal tedium of customs. In any case, Kimble was a secretary, not a valet. He'd dispensed with those ages ago in Vienna when he caught one out as a spy—for Austria, no less.

And there was little help to be found in the house because Hackwell had sent most of his servants off to have Christmas with their families.

He chuckled. Unconventional, Hackwell was, and his lady too, apparently, though Virgil had not had the pleasure of meeting her, and wasn't likely to, under the circumstances.

The old butler had put him in a room fronting the square, the heavy curtains and thick glazing still leaking in traffic noise, but never mind. He generally drank his way to sleep, anyway.

Murmuring voices were barely audible in the corridor. Hackwell had greeted him at the front door, threatening to send up a repast, and Virgil would have none of it. A night of drinking with his old commander would be just the thing, for both of them, probably. Hackwell had looked none too composed before running off to check on his lady.

Virgil limped to the door and stepped out. At the other end of the corridor, the butler was ushering a guest—a woman—into a chamber.

The skin on Virgil's neck prickled, and when she cast a glance back in profile, his breath caught. Her bonnet obstructed all but a straight nose, full lips, and a determined chin.

She was the right height, the right stature also. Before he could see more, Alton blocked his view, and the door closed on her.

He shook his head. The dress, dark, plain, and ugly, was wrong. His sister's companion had always favored more colorful dresses.

How very odd.

Hackwell's ancient retainer hurried over. "Is there aught that you need, milord?"

"Thank you, I am well settled. I see there is another guest."

The butler inclined his head. "That is the midwife."

"Indeed." He swallowed a smile and went to find the master of the house. Leave it to Hackwell to give the midwife a better room than a marquess.

Annabelle Beauverde, Lady Hackwell, opened the bedchamber door herself and pulled Ameline into as much of a hug as she could manage around her great swollen belly.

"My water has burst," she said, "and the pain is coming at regular intervals. And I am pacing, as you advised me to do."

The pain etched on her ladyship's face drove away all of Ameline's own worries. She had a knack for this, even Mrs. Crawford had said so. Here was a woman who needed her, and here she would be, and stay, until—please, God—the child was safely delivered and the mother in good health.

Lord Hackwell slipped an arm around his wife's shoulder. "Shall I stay? Do you not think she should lie down, Mrs. Dawes? Can all of this walking be good for her?" He ran his free hand through his hair.

His *trembling* free hand.

Ameline glanced around the room. Mary stood nearby wringing her own shaking hands.

Husbands generally made everyone more nervous and got in the way.

Ameline infused her smile with confidence. "Yes, I shall have you lie down now, my lady, so I can examine you. Mary, I will need your help with that. Lord Hackwell, if you could but just have Alton see that the kitchen has started the kettles boiling?"

He tugged his wife to him and kissed her tenderly. Ameline's eyes clouded and she turned away, setting out her instruments, trying to ignore his whispered endearments.

A new mother was blessed to have a man who cared so.

She heard Lady Hackwell's sharp intake of breath and turned to see her clutching her husband's arm.

His jaw tightened and his face paled. "I'm staying, love."

"Mary." Ameline signaled the maid, who hurried over. "My lord, the pain is quite normal. It is merely the body pushing the baby out, and it takes quite a bit of it to accomplish the task. Did not Mrs. Crawford explain? There now, my lady, Mary will help you to the bed, and I'll have a look at this wee one."

When Hackwell stayed frozen, she leaned closer. "Sir."

His gaze tracked the maid leading his wife to the big tester bed.

"My lord." Ameline edged even closer. "Your nerves will make this harder for her," she whispered.

"Ameline is right," Lady Hackwell called, her voice surprisingly strong. "I shall be fine. Don't worry, Steven. Go and chat with Lord Wallenford."

Wallenford. The room around went as grey, as if the fog had been sucked in through the fireplace. Ameline blinked away black spots and clutched the edge of a nearby table, her heart pounding wildly.

When she'd recovered her breath, Lord Hackwell was gone, and two pairs of eyes watched her, startled and round.

Heat rose in her, and she forced her hands to unclench. She must pull herself together. *Her* nerves would make everything harder. Beastly Wallenford didn't matter. Only Lady Hackwell and her babe mattered.

Wallenford was a guest of the Hackwells—a friend of the Hackwells. Oh, yes, he was very good at making friends, very personable, very kind. She must do her job, and then she and her girls would leave, as quickly and quietly as possible.

CHAPTER TWO

LADY HACKWELL CLOSED HER EYES AND slumped between Mary and Jenny, face dripping, hair falling loose at her shoulders.

Ameline mopped gently at her patient's face. "You're doing just as you ought," she said, mustering a reassuring tone, though in truth, she was a bit worried. Instead of increasing in frequency, the last few pains had slowed.

"Let's have you stretch out and I'll examine you again." She went to the basin and found the water not just tepid, but murky. *Where is that blasted girl with the water?*

She took a deep breath. "Jenny, what could be keeping the maid? It's been a good thirty minutes since you ran down there."

"One of the girls and the footman is in with the children. It's but one girl, Cook, and Alton, and them's busy getting together a tray their lordships ordered."

Jenny had connived a way to be in the birthing room, and Ameline was glad of it. Apparently though, the kitchen staff gave Lord Hackwell's needs precedence over Jenny's instructions.

"You go, Ameline," Lady Hackwell wheezed out. "I'll just have a wee rest 'til the next pain, and Mary will help me with a sip of the caudle."

"Ach, I fear it's gone cold also," Mary said. "Do go, Mrs. Dawes. You've not had even five minutes."

"They'll listen to you, Mrs. Dawes," Jenny said.

Lady Hackwell sent her a tired smile.

Fatigue crept over her and she swallowed it down, studying the woman in her care. If the pains continued to slow, she'd send word to Mrs. Crawford. Her bad back notwithstanding, Mrs. Crawford would come, and if need be, she'd secure the best accoucheur in London for Lady Hackwell.

"Go," Lady Hackwell said. "Visit the water closet. Whip Alton into shape. We'll wait right here for you."

She took a deep breath, clearing her head. "Right, then," she said, and hurried out.

"Devil take it, Major—er, Hackwell, can you not sit down?" Virgil poured out the last drops of brandy and handed them to his friend. "That's the end of it."

Hackwell tossed back the drink, and paced to the window. The dark curtains had been pulled closed against the London night. He raked them back to look out. "It's been hours," he muttered. "How long do these things take?"

"Hours and more hours, I hear." Virgil glanced at the empty bottle and the tray littered with dishes. "Come, let's play another hand and I'll beat you again."

He'd deemed it wise to lay out his own topic later, when Hackwell was less distracted. And so, they'd played endless games of vingt-un and drunk their way through the open bottle of brandy, discussing the years since they'd last seen each other.

Hackwell grunted but came and plopped down. "This will be you some day, Wallenford. You'll have to marry and go through this."

He smiled and dealt cards. "It's all my mother writes about. 'Come home and marry.' She dearly wants grandchildren."

Hackwell rewarded him with a chuckle. "Worried you'd bring home some Austrian?" He threw out a card.

"An opera singer disguised as a grand duchess."

Hackwell whooped. "By God, I don't envy you marching down the lines at Almack's checking how straight a girl's back is and the size of her decolla—"

"Dowry." He laughed and Hackwell joined him. "There now, you've won this hand, Major. All this talk of matrimony distracted me."

"Well, let me badger you more. What lucky young miss do you have in your sights? Perhaps Bella and I can help, though I must say, we are not considered good *ton*."

He thought of the midwife's profile. He'd spotted *her* in every city he'd visited—only to be disappointed when the girl had been too tall, or too short, or too anything but her.

"Or I suppose you want to look over the season's latest offerings."

"Not at all," Virgil said. "I know exactly the girl I want to marry. I just have to find her."

"Well now, here's a distracting story. I'm all ears."

"Yes, well, I thought perhaps you might be able to help, having sleuthed out your brother's killer."

Hackwell frowned.

"She lived with the family as a companion. After I went up to London to fetch news of Boney's escape, she left."

"Hell and damnation, man. She's the one who sent you that infernal letter that launched you into a three day binge."

He shook his head. "No." At least, not exactly. It had only been her name on the signature line. "She left without a character. My man of business traced her as far as London."

Hackwell tapped the table, pursing his lips. "Pretty?"

"Yes."

"No character, and in London. You realize the odds are good she may have had to make her way—"

"On her back. I know. That alone wouldn't stop me. I owe her."

"You compromised her?"

I loved her.

His heartbeat quickened. At least there'd been no accusation in Hackwell's tone. "Yes. Not my finest hour."

Except, in spite of Dulciana's death, in spite of his mother's intractable sadness, and his brother's bullying, it had been the finest few weeks of his life. Because of her.

"By God, we'll find her. If anyone can find a lost woman in London, it's my Bella."

A muffled cry filtered through the ceiling. Hackwell jumped out of his seat.

"Why not go check on her again, Major?" Hackwell had made three forays into the labor room.

"And have Mrs. Dawes toss me out of my own bedchamber again?" He looked at his empty tumbler. "Blast it, Wallenford, where are all my servants?"

Their last two tugs on the bell pull had gone unanswered. He stood and saluted. "I'll make a sortie to the kitchens for you, Major."

Hackwell stopped short and grinned. "Well, hell, Wallenford. I like the idea of a marquess waiting on me. Break down the door of my butler's pantry if you must, and bring back some bottles."

Virgil grabbed a candle and found his way to the servants' staircase, his bad leg barely paining him. Well, and that was the power of brandy.

Except for an occasional muffled shout, the house was understandably quiet. Hackwell had lost track of the hour, and most of the skeleton staff should be abed. Those who were not were most likely engaged with helping in the birthing chamber. Even he, a bachelor, could work that out.

One floor above the kitchens, he heard voices and saw a light.

"There now, 't'will be soon, Alton, and all will be well."

Virgil's foot paused above the stair and he gripped the banister. The woman's soothing tones had reached up to warm him in a familiar way.

"Have more brought up as soon as possible."

She was ascending the stairs toward him.

He blew out his candle and stepped down.

Ye gods, but her ladyship needed more maids, and a couple more footmen with both arms and both legs, at least for this type of fetching and carrying.

Ameline chided herself for being insensitive and balanced the steaming bucket. She set down the lamp momentarily to gather her skirts, along with the lamp handle.

A pair of men's boots moved into view and the lamp bobbled. Fine boots they were.

She sighed, gritting her teeth. Lord Hackwell's visits had unnerved his lady, and Ameline had counseled him to leave.

Very well, she'd thrown him out, once almost literally. He would wonder what *she* was doing below stairs. He might send for the accoucheur he was mumbling about, and his lady would not like it.

"I've just popped down to the kitchen for a word with Alton, my lord," she said. "All is going well, except he's a bit short on staff."

"We have noticed that."

The skin on her back rippled and she shivered. This wasn't Hackwell—it was *him*.

Panic flared in her and her hands and ankles began to tingle. He carried no light. She let her own lantern dip lower and stepped to one side. What was he doing on the servants' staircase in the middle of the night?

If he saw her, he *would* remember her, but he would not *want* to, unless he would think to *befriend* her again. Heat flamed in her.

She took in a breath. "Let me pass, *Lord Hackwell*," she said.

"Let me carry that bucket for you."

"No." She forced in another breath, willing herself to speak calmly. "That is, no thank you. I shall send a servant for you when it is time."

Footsteps scurried on the stairs. "Mrs. Dawes?" Jenny called, breathless.

Her heart raced again. She'd tarried too long in the kitchen. "I'll be right—"

Heat touched her hand as the bucket came out. The lantern, too, lifted higher, and she looked up into the face of Lord Virgil Radcliffe, now the latest Lord Wallenford.

"*Mrs. Dawes*?" His eyes widened and then narrowed, and his lips curved down.

Anger spiked in her. "*Lord Wallenford*."

He moved down to the step below her, putting them at eye level, and crowded her against the hand rail.

"Give me the bucket, sir. I can manage quite well without your help." Quite, quite well.

"Can you, indeed?" he drawled, sounding just like his brother the day he'd sacked her.

Blast him. Blast the Wallenfords. Blast the Hackwells. "Alton has a bottle set out. Best go and fetch it."

His lips quirked.

She gritted her teeth. "Give me the blasted bucket, Virgil."

"Mrs. Dawes?" Jenny stepped closer and reached for the bucket handle. "Begging your pardon, but she must hurry, my lord."

Virgil's gaze turned on the saucy maid, and Ameline silently saluted her. Jenny had survived as a child in the rookeries—no mere marquess would frighten her.

"Very well," he said. "Carry the bucket for the *lady*."

Her hand fisted around the lantern handle and she saw the candle he fumbled with, still dripping wet wax.

He'd deliberately snuffed it out. He'd known it was her. He'd known about her. And how?

"We'll talk later, Mrs. Dawes."

A loud moan snaked its way down the stairs from the upper floors, driving out all thoughts of Wallenford.

*****

"Eat, Hackwell." Virgil began filling a plate from the dishes he'd helped Alton carry up from the kitchen. "You must eat, else you'll be bowsy when you greet your heir."

Hackwell grunted and took a bite. "Did you wake Cook, Wallenford? Don't tell me you and Alton pulled all these dishes together yourself."

Virgil forced a laugh. "You'd be surprised. I believe all of your servants are in the kitchen boiling water for Mrs. Dawes." He poured himself a brandy. "Who, by the way, I met on the staircase, on her way up from dressing down the staff for not being quick enough to answer her demands."

Hackwell lifted an eyebrow.

Finally, he'd managed to distract Hackwell, and not by what he'd said. The man was too perceptive by half.

"A memorable encounter, I take it?"

A memorable encounter that stirred other memories. The dim light of the lantern had only enhanced her full lips and dark, intense eyes. And the more he thought about it, she'd filled out, too, from the underfed waif to a woman with more generous curves under her serviceable gown.

"Pour me some of that." Hackwell slid over his glass. "A fetching young woman, is she not? She's the midwife, as you've probably deduced. We could have brought in one of these fashionable man-midwives, but I'm not fond of another man fiddling about in my wife's privates, and as Bella said, one wonders how someone who's not been through the experience can be totally effective.

And anyway, Mrs. Dawes is one of my wife's bluestocking friends. I quite like her."

The rambling words clanged about in Virgil's brain. Ameline, a bluestocking, a midwife, and friend to a countess.

And married. Perhaps she'd just adopted that term of address in the course of her duties.

She couldn't be married. It wasn't possible, was it? Not without a dowry, and Ameline had never had one, had she? But of course there could be other men besides him who'd take her without a dowry. Mr. Dawes must care for her.

Like *he* cared for her. And she was supposed to be *his*. "Where is Mr. Dawes while his wife is running about birthing babies?"

Hackwell scratched the dark stubble on his chin. He'd loosened his neck cloth and coats, the expectant father all at his leisure. "Dead. Bella said she's a widow."

His body heated and thrummed. Dead.

"If you can't find your missing woman, are you interested? She's gentry stock, I believe, but in the conventional order of things, beneath a marquess."

Heat spiked in him and his lungs filled again. Dead, dead, the husband was dead. Ameline was widowed, his missing woman. He could have her beneath him again.

He'd never been one for whores and actresses, and even after his injuries had healed, he'd not had a woman since Ameline—no one had appealed.

But *she'd* found someone. *She'd* married.

Through the tangle of thoughts, another muffled sound reached them, and then a cry, like a cat mewling.

Hackwell shot out of his seat, tightening his neck cloth, and began pacing.

The knot was crooked and the uneven sides of his waistcoat flapped about. "You might want to shave before you greet your lady wife," Virgil said. "Or at least button that coat properly."

Hackwell waved a hand. "For the love of God, distract me, Wallenford. It's the only reason I'm allowing you to stay here during this infernal ordeal. Yes, I'll help you find your woman, but why are you in London in my townhouse instead of your own?"

He groaned. He'd been airing his troubles with solicitors and money lenders. He'd hoped to avoid discussing them with peers. But Hackwell had been his commander during his brief military career, and then his friend while they were both in Vienna. He could be trusted. "The usual reasons."

Hackwell inclined his head to the door and began fumbling buttons. "Estate in disarray?"

The man had an uncanny ability to hold more than one target in his sights. "Yes. My father and brother didn't manage as well as I'd thought."

"Been through the same thing. You shall have my help—mine, my wife's and my steward's, if you want it."

"Good of you, Hackwell."

"Yes, well, good that you came back. It's hard to manage finding a woman and fixing an estate from the Continent. And as you say, your mother has been hounding you to return."

"Yes." His mother and others. The last letter had come from his brother's former betrothed, Caroline Jermyn, urging him to return for his mother's sake. That letter had done the trick, though not for the reasons Caroline had put forward. "I've stayed away as long as I could. Now I'm rearranging debts and pursuing some other avenues." Footsteps shuffled in the corridor, the sound growing louder. "We have minerals to exploit, and we're in dire need of some new agricultural practices."

Hackwell nodded as he moved to the door, opening it before the messenger could knock.

A maid, an older one than the girl he'd seen on the stairs, bobbed a curtsy. "It's a girl, milord. And Mrs. Dawes, she says to tell you she's a healthy mite, and that her ladyship is well, and she will send for you as soon as her ladyship and the room are cleaned up and put right."

Hackwell whooped and clamped hands on the maid's shoulders, just short of a hug. The shocked woman gave him a lopsided grin and ran off.

Virgil filled their two glasses again and met Hackwell halfway, raising a toast. "To your new daughter. Have you come up with a name?"

"Little Lady some-such, devil take it. I shall let Bella name her." He smiled broadly. "A girl."

"Disappointed it's not a boy?"

"Hell, no, man. You're not one of those jackanapes clamoring for an heir to safeguard the entail, are you, Wallenford?"

"No. My mother is doing all of the clamoring. Ends every letter with a reminder."

"Does your missing woman have money? She could solve two problems."

He groaned. "Not you, too."

Hackwell laughed. "Bella's money saved the tenants' roofs, but even without it I'd have married her and got out my ladder and hammer. And she can give me ten girls and I'll be happy. I had no mother or sisters or even girl cousins growing up, and now I'm raising my nephew and brother. You at least had your mother to bring a feminine presence into your life."

"I had a sister, also."

"Devil take it. I didn't know that."

"She was...never quite up to the family standards. Kept her hidden away in the country. Dulciana died a few months before my brother."

Hackwell's head shot up. "Dulciana?"

"That was her name."

"An unusual name." Hackwell's eyes narrowed.

Virgil's neck itched, and an ache started around his heart. Dulciana had been the family's dark secret, the imperfect child stowed away in the nursery. His twin, damaged at birth. He was never supposed to talk of her. "I suppose so."

A tap at the door brought news that her ladyship was ready to receive her husband's visit.

Hackwell waved a hand at the still loaded trays. "I'll leave that feast to you, Wallenford."

Virgil took the bottle and a glass and retired to a dark corner, prepared to drink his way through the rest of the night. The mention of his sister, and the appearance of Ameline, a widowed Ameline, set his spirits dancing between melancholy and anger and, truth to tell, hope.

He'd expected to have to look harder for her. He'd expected to find her at some godforsaken manor, wrangling brats, or wiping an old lady's arse. Or worse, flat on her back in one of the houses in St. James's.

He'd not seen her since his brother, the last marquess, sent him off to London to find out about Bonaparte's escape from Elba.

To get him out of the way. After he left, Ameline had packed her bags and departed without giving a reason. So Virgil had been told.

He'd written to his mother for news, and enlisted Baker, the family's harried steward and Virgil's childhood friend, to find Ameline while he went off to Belgium with Wellington's crew. And then, Ameline's letter had arrived, enclosed in one from his brother, telling him not just goodbye, but good riddance.

It had taken him three wasted years to know who had written that goodbye, years of running away, years of Ameline finding and perhaps loving another man, a man who was not Virgil. The thought raised an ache in all his mangled parts.

He lifted his glass and paused. Perhaps there was a better fix tonight than getting himself foxed. She was free now, and so was he.

The study door opened and a figure slipped in.

Virgil bobbled his glass, sloshing brandy onto the table, and setting it down quietly.

CHAPTER THREE

AMELINE HURRIED TO THE LADEN TABLE, pulled off her cap, and massaged her temples. As births went, this one had been blessedly routine. A child came on God's time, and the journey exhausted the mother and the midwife, the mother's labor wrenching Ameline's insides as if she were experiencing childbirth again herself.

She pulled over a plate and filled it, grateful to take this bone-weary repast alone in the quiet of Hackwell's study. A branch of candles illuminated the table, but outside the circle of light all was shadowed. The smell of leather bound books, tobacco, and the low fire reached her, bringing back memories of home, and the room where her father secluded himself when he needed solitude.

Her fork clacked on the plate, her knife sawing ineffectually, until she abandoned politeness and picked up a piece of ham in her fingers, taking a large bite and chewing. "Mmm, that's good," she mumbled around a mouthful, a chuckle rising within her. She could never be so improper around the children. *A lady is a lady, even in private.* She'd used her mother's gentle rebuke on her own girls, as well as the girls at the children's home.

She squeezed her eyes shut. She'd not been a lady in private with Virgil Radcliffe. In fact, that lapse had sealed her future. If not for the kindness of others, and if not for Mr. Dawes...well, gentry or no, she was no longer a lady, and in this quiet moment didn't have to put on high and mighty manners for Dulciana and Emily's sake.

A flash of movement in the corner sent the hair on her neck dancing and her ham clattering against the utensils.

Oh God, no.

A shadow rose, took form and approached the table. She wiped her hands and reached for her cap.

"Leave it, Ameline."

Virgil's rich baritone sent chills down her spine. He'd always claimed to love her mousy brown hair, seeing hints of gold that no one else could.

Hands shaking, she pulled the cap over her head ungracefully, shoving loose locks under. "Go to the study, he said," she croaked. "Have something to eat, he said." Suspicion threaded through her, but she quickly pushed it away. Hackwell had been muddle-headed, not manipulative, sending her here. "I shall leave you in peace, *Lord* Wallenford."

She tried to push back her chair, but his hand clamped down on the back of it.

Her pulse quickened. If she but leaned back, the hard knots of his knuckles might ease the tight fibers around her spine.

And the thought made her face heat. Virgil's power over her hadn't abated. He could still reduce her to a besotted fool.

No. She squeezed her eyes shut and remembered her own hours and hours of wrenching labor birthing twins. She was strong. She could master this. She would not be left alone again in a puddle of foolish sensibility.

"Stay. Finish eating. *Mrs.* Dawes."

She opened her eyes and let out a breath. A hint of anger had colored Virgil's tone, and her nerves prickled. He'd never been like his father or his brother. He wouldn't have raised a hand to a woman before. What sort of man was he now?

Mrs. Dawes. It was the *Mrs.* that had his voice breaking. Her marriage upset him. While he traipsed about the world, he thought she would have waited, penniless and friendless, raising his children.

Her thoughts flew to the nursery, where the girls would be rising soon. She clutched the edge of the table. How much had Virgil learned about her and her girls from Hackwell?

Seconds ticked by. Finally, he released her chair, pulling another over and seating himself next to her, propped on an elbow, his green gaze making her skin prickle.

She turned what she intended to be a defiant look upon him, and her stomach fluttered. On the stairway, she hadn't had enough time or light for a good look. Three years of battle, and serving the Crown, and inheriting a title and all that great responsibility had carved lines into Virgil's face and made him even more impossibly handsome. His dark hair curled and tangled, his beard sprouted in a dark scruff, and his green eyes flashed darkly in the candlelight. Blackbeard, his sister Dulciana used to call him with a giggle, raking her fingernails over his jaw.

As Ameline had also done.

The knot in her stomach moved up to her throat. *I want you still. Even though you deserted me.* She grabbed a glass of dark liquid, swallowed and choked as it burned through her.

She took in a deep breath. "The Marquess of Wallenford."

"Mrs. Dawes, midwife. He leaned close. "A squire's daughter, working as a midwife."

"Yes, indeed. I'm quite good at it, and I like it."

He flinched, and she realized, he did not like being the marquess, and that was not surprising. Virgil had always had more capacity for fun and adventure than the two dour men who'd preceded him in the title. His traveling the last three years must have fitted him better, even if the duties hadn't.

What if he hadn't gone off? What if his brother hadn't died? What if they'd found a way together?

She tried to shrug off those thoughts, but he pursed his lips, and warmth shot through her center. He'd kissed her with those lips, everywhere.

"You're very lucky then," he said.

Lucky? How was she lucky? She, a gentleman's daughter, had struggled through birthing twins. Bastards. This man's girls.

Tears threatened, and she blinked them back. She had beautiful girls, and perhaps he was right. She'd been blessed beyond belief to find women who'd helped her. There'd been a trace of envy in his voice, and why? He'd inherited a title, and he'd fallen in with Hackwell as a friend, and Hackwell was known to be a decent sort.

"And you're a marquess. Shall I offer condolences or congratulations? Perhaps both." She pushed the plate back. "And now, I shall leave you in peace."

He dragged the plate close and picked up her utensils. "Stay, Ameline. Talk to me." He sawed at the meat, carving it into small pieces. "These are very good nibbles, as you used to say to my sister. And you're very hungry."

She swallowed a lump. She was. Or, she had been. He stabbed a morsel of meat and lifted it to her. "Take a bite."

The air around her quaked with the scent of the meat and the essence of Virgil, a scent that defied conscious awareness. She accepted the bite and slid it from the tines of the fork, chewing slowly, her heart beating a fierce tattoo, her belly rumbling with carnal hunger that rested somewhat lower than her stomach.

"When did you last eat?" he asked, bringing her attention higher.

The meat clogged her throat, and she choked again.

He handed her a cup of tea. "Drink this. Though I'm afraid it's gone cold."

I haven't.

Another piece of meat stood ready in his steady hand for transport into her trembling mouth.

"Your last meal, Ameline?" he asked, sternly.

"This morning." She said.

"What? You had no meal before leaving your, er, lodgings, to come here?"

His gaze fixed her. He was fishing—he thought she lived in London.

Her mind jumped ahead and sent her heart plummeting. Hackwell would tell him where she lived, and if he wished to bother her, he jolly well would ride out to Sussex and do so.

The meat she'd just swallowed formed a lump in her chest. And what of her girls? He was a marquess. No matter how she declared Mr. Dawes their father, one could look at them and know they were Virgil's. And once he met them, once he saw them, he *would* try to take them.

She waved his fork away. "I reside in the country."

"Please eat, Ameline." His touch on her arm sent shivers through her.

She pulled away. This could not be. "I've lost my appetite." Such a liar, she was. "If I'd known you would be here, I'd have insisted Lady Hackwell call in someone else to attend her."

"Why?"

"I have no wish to see you, ever again." That was only a half-lie. She wished to do more than see him—she wished to thrash him for what he'd done to her, for the way he'd promised to help and then left.

"Tell me of your husband."

When she looked, Virgil's face had gone tight, his jaw locked, and what she saw calmed her. He was not so at ease this night either.

"My husband...is no more." That was less of a lie than saying he was dead.

"You're a widow?"

She nodded. "And now, I will leave." She pushed back her chair and stood.

His hand shot out and took hers, sending electricity up her arm, like the lightening striking Mr. Franklin's kite.

"I don't care about your title, Wallenford. I won't be bullied." *Or seduced. Dear God.*

"Is that what I'm doing?" A grin spread across his face, Virgil's grin, playful and free, and for a moment she was back in his sister's set of nursery rooms watching him tease Dulciana.

He stroked his thumb over the back of her hand. "Oh, I suppose I am. And what good is a title if you can't bully people, Ameline. That was always Father's rule."

He stood, keeping hold of her hand. "We were friends once, Ameline. Equals."

Equals? A marquess's younger brother and a hired companion? Well, perhaps they had been equally bullied. He was sent off to war, and she was just sent off. They'd both landed on their feet, but in very different worlds. "You were always Lord Virgil to me."

"You were to take care of Granny after Dulciana died. Why did you leave, Ameline?" His gaze pinned her again.

Her chest ached. He didn't know what had happened. Or, he did and this was some sort of test.

The sort of test she refused to take part in. "It does not matter." She tugged at her hand and his grip tightened. "I had a new opportunity. Let me go, Wallenford." His frown deepened but his grip relaxed and she pulled her hand away. "Now, I really must leave."

She kept to a normal pace, but as soon as the door closed on her she ran up the stairs to her room.

Virgil watched Ameline's departure, gripping the chair like an anchor to keep from following her. He would get her to talk to him, but not tonight. She was shocked, tired, and probably still famished.

Now that he'd found her, he'd need time to woo her. How long would a visiting midwife stay? At least overnight.

He poured a drink, looked at it, and set it down. He could bribe a servant to tell him if she left. In any case, she would stay at least one more day to look after her patient, and probably longer.

And blast it, his other infernal business would keep him tied up tomorrow and the next day.

His mind too filled with plotting to sit quietly and drink, he blew out the candles and headed up to his chamber, so close to hers. If she ran, would it be back to her own home? Tomorrow, he'd work in a few moments alone with Hackwell and find out just where in the country he'd found Ameline Dawes.

CHAPTER FOUR

"SHE IS BEAUTIFUL, IS SHE NOT?"

Lord Hackwell rocked the white bundle in his arms while four pairs of eyes looked on. After a day and a night of some rest, Lady Hackwell felt well enough to entertain the younger members of her household.

The boys jostled each other, but Dee climbed up on the sofa and tucked herself close to Lord Hackwell, sending a spurt of guilt through Ameline.

Her girls had never known a father, an uncle, or an older brother. The staff of the children's home was primarily women. The man engaged for the heavy work, and the vicar who came in once a week had to be shared among all the children. When Lord Hackwell visited, his kind good looks and open hearty manner drew in everyone who knew him, most especially the children.

"You have done well, my dear." Hackwell beamed a smile at his wife, who returned his warmth.

"I shall come down for tea this evening, I think," Lady Hackwell said.

"What say you, Mrs. Dawes? Is my wife ready to roam about the house?"

Ameline stalled, tucking a pillow behind her ladyship. "Generally, the rule is to keep the new mother in bed, but many women don't have that luxury, and some don't care to lie about. Do you feel up to a trip to the drawing room, my lady?"

Lady Hackwell sat all the way up, swung her legs from the bed and stood. "Yes, indeed. And you children can come down later. We shall have a family day. It is Christmas Eve, isn't it?"

And thank God for that. She was another day closer to leaving. Ameline straightened the bedding, while Lady Hackwell kissed cheeks and sent the children off to the nursery.

This home was generous and warm, yet Ameline could not wait to depart. The baby was healthy, as was her mother. As soon as she'd assisted Mrs. Crawford with one more birth, she could leave.

Lady Hackwell sat down by her husband. "Wallenford is out again?" she asked. "Does he not know it is Christmas?"

Wallenford, Wallenford. Lady Hackwell had been prattling about his comings and goings, while Ameline walked on pins and needles and kept the girls out of his sight.

"Yes," Hackwell said. "And likely to be out again late tonight. The perfect guest, eh? Though not nearly as helpful as Mrs. Dawes has been."

I'm a servant, not a guest. She bit back the words. The Hackwells had put her up in a guest chamber with a bed bigger than any she'd ever slept in. It was endearingly generous, if she ignored the knowledge that Virgil was housed at the other end of the corridor. "You have been most kind, my lord. Dulciana, Emma, and I are grateful."

"Dulciana." He rubbed at his chin. "She'll lead some man a merry chase someday. And by the by, Wallenford mentioned he had a sister named Dulciana."

Her stomach sank. It was an unusual name, and the wheedling tone told her he was prying. When she looked up, they were both watching her.

She came round the bed to stand before them. "Yes, he did. Lady Wallenford hired me as a companion—a nurse really—for her daughter. She was…intellectually impaired, a child, though not in years, and yet had the sweetest spirit of any person I've ever met. She d-died. My daughters carry her name, Dulciana Emma. I would ask that you not t-tell…" she cleared her throat, inwardly cursing the way her voice shook, "that you not discuss my daughters with Lord Wallenford, as he would not appreciate my gesture. His sister's death quite affected him."

"Will he not be honored by your thoughtfulness?" Hackwell asked. "I would be."

Lady Hackwell sent her husband a look. "Ameline will know best, my dear. Though, perhaps...my husband might be right. Wallenford may wish for the chance to reminisce with you about his sister."

She tried to swallow around the lump in her throat. "Perhaps. But I would not. I should like that part of my past to remain in the past." She took a breath. "The years before I settled at Longview were not the easiest. I hope you will understand."

"We quite understand." Lady Hackwell patted her husband's knee. "Still, I would like you to have tea with us this afternoon. Wallenford will not be about, and we need to bring Christmas to this home."

Later, after they'd had tea and sent the three younger children back to the nursery, Ameline sat in the drawing room with the Hackwells and Thomas around a table spread with biscuits, cheeses, and the ribbons and green boughs they were tying into wreathes. A fire blazed in the hearth, and the baby slept peacefully in a cradle at Lady Hackwell's feet.

Alton broke the peace, carrying in a visitor's card.

Lady Hackwell scanned the card and frowned up at her husband. "We must send her away." She passed the card to him.

He stood and straightened his coats. "I'll deal with it." But before he could take a step, the door opened, and a visitor stepped in, sending Ameline's heart into a frenzy.

Lady Wallenford, Virgil's mother, glided in, her skirts rustling, and the feathers at the crown of her bonnet waving. "Oh, I do apologize, Lord Hackwell, but I've come to see my son." Her gaze circled the room and landed on Ameline.

Eyes widening, the older lady's face drained of all color.

Ameline rose and tottered against the table. Behind Lady Wallenford stood Caroline Jermyn.

"Miss Illington." Lady Wallenford sounded breathless. "What are you doing here?"

"She's Mrs. Dawes," Thomas said.

"Thank you, Thomas, for making introductions." Lord Hackwell's tone was bland. "Lady Wallenford, You may or may not find Virgil at White's or Brooks's or Boodle's. Or he may well be with his solicitor. I could not be sure as I am only the man providing him lodgings. But now you are here, we are having a family day with our dear friend, Mrs. Dawes, preparing for Christmas. Please sit and join us. And this is my brother, Thomas. Thomas, run down to the kitchen and tell Cook we need a fresh pot of tea and more biscuits. Have you heard our happy news, Lady Wallenford? My wife has just been delivered of a baby girl."

"Which explains my *deshabille*," Lady Hackwell said. "And why we are so at our leisure."

Lady Wallenford's face brightened. "Congratulations. When was the dear child born?"

"Why, only the day before yesterday."

The older lady's mouth dropped. "And your accoucheur allows you—"

"Heavens, no. Dear Mrs. Dawes was my midwife. And I feel quite well."

Lady Wallenford turned a startled gaze on Ameline.

She stifled a groan. The story of the gauche Lady Hackwell would be all over Mayfair in hours, but her benefactress only smiled pleasantly.

"We stood ready of course to call upon a qualified surgeon of my acquaintance," Ameline said.

"Not the same qualified medical men as attended the Princess last year," Lord Hackwell said wryly. Even at the far reaches of England, everyone had heard that under the care of the leading doctors of the realm Princess Charlotte had died in childbirth.

Ameline decided to hold her tongue.

Not even their careful social masks could conceal the voyage of emotions in both visitors' faces as they absorbed the mention of Ameline as a *dear friend*, and then her role as Lady Hackwell's attending midwife, but they managed to settle into benign smiles. Polite introductions were made all around and both ladies sat down, carefully ignoring the room's chaos, and of course, Ameline.

She had no wish to be thrown into tea with them. Nor would she clear places at the table for them. They'd ruined the day's fun. "I'll just go and check on Thomas," Ameline said.

Lady Hackwell's hand clasped hers, managing to transmit calm. "Sit, my dear. Cook will stop him from eating all the biscuits."

Ameline sat.

"Lord Wallenford said you were remaining in the country, my lady. Steven, we will just have to pack up your friend and send him to his own townhouse."

"No, no," Lady Wallenford said. "I'm staying in town with Caroline's parents, Sir Henry and his lady. I merely wanted to surprise Wallenford." She sent Ameline a pointed look. "He'll be so happy to hear that Caroline is in town."

"And Mama has plenty of room for Wallenford," Caroline said. "We should love to have him be our guest."

So that was the game afoot. Lady Wallenford was matching Virgil up with Caroline.

Anger spiked in her, and something greener. It was so unworthy, and she had no right. Of course Caroline would be matched up with Virgil now that he'd returned. It was the most natural assumption.

She took a deep breath and tried for a polite tone. "My condolences, Miss Jermyn," she said. "My condolences on the loss of your fiancé, the late Lord Wallenford. My condolences to the both of you."

"Yes, well, Caroline's period of mourning is long over, and it is time to move on, is it not? Like a daughter to me, is Caroline. So very dear."

"You were his brother's fiancée, Miss Jermyn?" Hackwell asked. "Well then, I suppose you're like a sister to Wallenford. Yes, yes, I will let him know his mother and er—sister are in town."

Caroline's eyes flashed, and a wild giggle started inside Ameline, but the squeeze of Lady Hackwell's hand pressed it back. Dear Lord, how she loved the Hackwells.

Lady Wallenford sat up straighter. "And so, you've had a daughter, Lord Hackwell? Well perhaps the next child will be a boy."

One of his eyebrows shot up. "I greatly value my daughter, I find." He smiled at his wife. "Perhaps especially as we have two boys underfoot now, my brother and my nephew, who we are raising. Should my lady give me ten more girls, I will not mind."

A bleating noise from the cradle brought Lady Wallenford's chin up, and as Lady Hackwell lifted her daughter and straightened the swaddling around her, the older lady's face softened.

She stood and moved closer. "She is beautiful."

"Would you like to hold her?" Lady Hackwell asked.

"Oh." Lady Wallenford took the child and cradled her, and Ameline's heart thudded. She'd seen this Lady Wallenford from time to time, in rare moments of laughter with her impaired daughter.

The lady wanted children in her life. The thought sent Ameline's pulse pounding again. She must get her girls out of here before either of the Wallenfords saw them, and took them.

And what of Caroline? If Virgil took Dee and Em and married Caroline, her girls would freeze from the lack of love.

And why wouldn't he marry Caroline? He'd always been considerate of his mother, and truth to tell, he'd been her favorite. If a marriage between him and Caroline was her fondest wish, he would certainly give in to the inevitable.

Before the tea could be delivered, Lady Wallenford handed back the babe, and the ladies left. When the door closed on them, Hackwell sat back and rubbed his chin, frowning. "I don't believe Wallenford has plans to marry that young lady. Shall we tell him about this visit? I suppose we must. He will want to know his mother has swept into town to corner him."

"He is your friend, my dear. But what to do you think, Ameline? You knew him before he inherited the title."

Her cheeks grew warm. She put her attention to cutting a length of ribbon. "It's none of my affair."

That wasn't a lie. The Wallenfords had cast her off, and their business was none of hers, nor would it be. Ever.

"No of course not," Lady Hackwell said. "But you can advise us. Does he have a *tendre* for the young lady?"

She pressed her lips together. Virgil had been sweet on Caroline when they were children, until the girl threw him over for his brother. "The Jermyn estate borders Wallenford's. It would be a suitable arrangement for both families. I believe she was raised to be a marchioness." She bit her lip. Caroline had shared that pronouncement with Virgil, who'd told it to Ameline, one afternoon. Virgil had laughed about it, and meant it, his jolly heart fully mended from what, after all, was only a minor disappointment.

"Was she?" Hackwell laughed. "And I suppose she'll settle for any marquess."

"The question is," Lady Hackwell said, "will any marquess settle for her? What do you think, Ameline?"

She forced a smile. "I think, my lady, I am out of my depth."

Lady Hackwell laughed. "I will say, Lady Wallenford looked shocked to see you here, and stunned that you are working as a midwife."

Ameline took a deep breath. "That was not exactly personal. Her daughter, Dulciana, was a twin to Lord Wallenford, born second after a long labor, with a midwife attending. She doesn't have a high regard for the profession." She set down her length of ribbon. "And now, I'll go and remove Thomas from the kitchens before there are no more biscuits left for the others when they wake from their naps."

Lady Hackwell exchanged a look with her husband. "Let him be. Cook will make more biscuits. While the girls are still napping, go and have a lie-down in your room. You must take advantage of my nursery staff until you return to Longview."

Happy for some time alone, Ameline paused on her floor and looked at the other bedchamber door. Virgil was out, would be for some time, but she couldn't rely on him staying away forever. Sooner or later, he would meet her girls, unless Ameline took them far, far away.

No. What was she thinking? Sooner or later, the girls *should* meet their father. But she'd much rather it be later.

She climbed the stairs all the way to the nursery.

It was dark outside, but not much past the town dinner hour, when Virgil slipped into the house and handed Alton his hat and gloves.

A loud squeal erupted from behind the closed drawing room door, followed by cackling laughter and the low rumble of Hackwell's voice.

The butler cleared his throat. "The family are hanging pine boughs and mistletoe, and having chocolate in the drawing room."

Longing spiked in him. He recalled a rare Christmas as a boy, when a kindly nursemaid had helped him and his sister Dulciana decorate the nursery. And with Ameline under the same roof, mistletoe made him yearn for other possibilities. "Perhaps I'll join them."

"I'll have a fresh pot sent up," the butler said, opening the drawing room door.

"No need." Virgil turned to wish him happy Christmas, and a small body crashed into him. He looked down, and his heart dropped.

CHAPTER FIVE

A LITTLE GIRL STARED UP AT HIM.

Dark-haired, round-faced, her eyes gleamed with interest and intelligence, eyes the same moss green as his own. She wore a tiny cinched robe and slippers the size of a doll's.

A balled up paper struck her and she flinched against him, clutching the tops of his boots.

"Got you, Dulciana," a boy cried.

The boy of perhaps ten hopped on one foot, and another child tackled him, a girl who looked just like the one wrapped around his legs.

His heart squeezed. *Dulciana.* His sister's face had been round, her hair dark, and her eyes the same color as his own. This child looked just like his sister, and the other girl very much so also.

They were twins.

The girl's mouth crumpled, the way his sister's had when their mother had ordered the pine boughs and ribbons removed from the nursery.

They made his sister sneeze, she'd said. After Mother had left, Virgil had crawled on Dulciana's bed and cried along with her.

He scooped this little girl up. "Dulciana, is it?" She was light as a feather, a child of two or possibly three. "And who is she?" He pointed at the other girl.

"That's Emma," the boy said.

Emma. Dulciana Emma. His sister's names. His senses dulled, thrummed, sharpened anew.

A much younger blond boy scooted over and stared up at Virgil.

"That's Robby. I'm Thomas," the older boy said.

Robby launched a crumpled paper at Emma, who squealed and collapsed to the floor.

"Come here, Emma," Virgil said.

She toddled over warily.

It was the same look he'd seen on Ameline's face in the study. And this little girl's eyes weren't green, but a dark brown, like Ameline's. He swallowed a lump.

"Come" He propped Dulciana on his hip and hoisted Emma up, his heart fair to bursting.

His mangled shoulder should ache from the weight of the tiny girl, but it didn't.

Candles brightened every corner of the room and a fire roared in the grate. Pine boughs tied with ribbon wreathed the mantel, adding to the festive scent. The boys rolled on the floor together in their nightshirts, giggling and tussling.

His gaze landed on Hackwell seated with a pretty dark-haired lady—his lady, surely—both of them silent, mouths agape, watching him.

Heart clanging, he fought for a breath. Speechless, were they? Well, why not? They'd not told him anything. Not one word. And yet, they *must* have known.

Ameline was not present. Yet these girls...Dulciana. He remembered Hackwell's look of surprise and his comment—*not a common name*.

They'd known, and withheld it from him, and now sat like two mummers.

Moments ticked by. Hackwell spoke, making introductions. His lady spoke. Virgil answered by rote.

What else had Hackwell said that other night? How could a midwife who'd not been through the pain be effective?

Tiny chilled hands flattened against his cheek, fingers rubbing along his rising stubble. Both pink bowed mouths had fallen open, the way his sister's used to do, but there was intelligence in their little faces, and curiosity as fingers swept along his jaw.

"Dulciana and Emma?" Virgil managed to keep his voice steady, his gaze flitting between both little girls. "You are twins?"

Dulciana's full lips quirked in the start of a smile. She had the purest white teeth, small and perfect.

"Well?" he asked.

"Yessss," she hissed.

"And what are your full names?"

"Dulciana and Emma Dawes."

Dulciana's rich, low voice stole his breath away.

Emma watched him, unblinking and intense, the quiet one. *Just like her mother.*

His heart raced. Hackwell said something, but he couldn't understand it. The bundles in his arms held all his interest, all his attention. "And how old are you, Dulciana and Emma Dawes?"

Dulciana's eyes brightened and she held up three fingers. "My birfday is Christmas."

Three. On December 25th.

His muddled mind ran through the calculation, the room glimmering and crashing around him.

Steady, Wallenford. "And aren't you big girls."

"I'm bigger." Dulciana sniffed, and swiped her hand across her nose.

"Are not," Emma said.

He bounced both of them higher, squashing a grin, vaguely hearing the boys' chatter, seeing Lady Hackwell rising. A maid took both girls from him, set them down, and with Lady Hackwell, led all the children away.

Twins. She'd had twins, all by herself. Who'd been with her? Who'd helped her? It should have been him, not some man named Dawes.

He blindly followed Hackwell to his study, found a chair, and took a shaky drink. Hackwell spoke and another man answered, and Virgil greeted Hackwell's steward, Bink Gibson, another old soldier. More friend than servant, he and Hackwell began to talk of politics and business, the words slowly making sense to Virgil.

The shock in him was lifting, and other emotions filled him—anger, and in no small part, shame. She'd had twins, and withheld the news. She'd gone off, ripe with two babies and birthed them all by herself. What the hell had happened at Willowbrook after he'd left? And why hadn't he tried harder to find her?

He tossed back drink after drink, contributing little to the talk.

When he went to pour another, the bottle was empty.

Hackwell pulled a bottle from a cabinet. "You are on the cut tonight, I see, Wallenford. I hope you've not had bad news today."

Bad news? Was more betrayal bad news? "I'll order you up a case at Berry's."

"No need for dramatics." Hackwell uncorked the fresh bottle. "You look like a man whose best horse has broken a leg. But Gibson and I are here to commiserate and give you advice. We'll cajole you to jolliness, if for no other reason than for the sake of the children. I believe Bella is planning something special for them tomorrow."

"You're spoiling the little hellions," Gibson said.

"Yes, well, we'll whip them into shape the rest of the year. But Mrs. Dawes's little girls turn three tomorrow. We must have a party."

Nine months to breed a child. Father had died in January, Dulciana on the February day when Bonaparte had escaped from Elba. And it was after that he and Ameline had begun their affair, and April when he'd gone up to London, and the

52

eighteenth of June—if he could but forget—when he'd had his first taste of bloody battle.

His fists curled around the arms of the chair. Unless Dulciana and Emma Dawes had come before time, they were his. Either way, Ameline had gone directly from Virgil's bed to Mr. Dawes's. And who the hell was this Mr. Dawes? There'd been no man by that name in the neighborhood.

"Tell me, Hackwell, about Mrs. Dawes's husband," he said.

Gibson stopped mid-sentence and both men stared at him. Devil take it, he'd interrupted them, and he didn't care.

Hackwell's gaze narrowed. Virgil locked eyes with him. Damn it, he outranked both men and he'd damn well bully them if he had to.

"Her man went off to Waterloo and died there," Gibson said. Hackwell turned a shocked gaze on him and the steward shrugged. "Heard it from your lady."

Her man died at Waterloo.

Virgil rose and went to the grate, staring into the burning coals. Dulciana and Emma Dawes had his sister's dark hair. Dulciana had his sister's eyes. *His* hair. *His* eyes. There'd been no Mr. Dawes before Virgil's brother had packed him off to London for news of Bonaparte's escape. Not long after that, his mother had sent word of Ameline's departure.

He'd left soon after to join the allied army gathering in Belgium.

"She wound up under Lady Hackwell's wing because the husband's family dismissed her, or some such."

"You're a fountain of knowledge, Gibson," Hackwell said. "It wasn't her comely appearance that led to your inquiries, was it?"

"I offered to make inquiries about a pension, is all. Lady H said she suggested it to Mrs. Dawes, but the lady wasn't interested and came close to tears every time she brought it up."

Gibson said his goodnights and left.

The family dismissed her. They'd been lovers for a month. He'd made promises, ones he very much intended to keep. And she'd crept off into the night, in a way a lesser man—and his family—would be grateful for.

Baker had made inquiries for him and traced her as far as London. Then, while he'd been sitting in Belgium trying to work out how to soldier, his brother's letter had enclosed a newly discovered note from Ameline that had made clear she'd no interest in him anymore.

A note designed to cut off his inquiries. What a fool he'd been.

"A coy one is our Bink Gibson," Hackwell said. "I rather thought Mrs. Dawes might be a good match for him, but I believe he might be getting ready to take up the sword again. He's been spending far too much time reading the news out of Punjab." Hackwell leaned back and put his feet up on the writing table. "Sit down, man. You look like you've seen a ghost."

Hackwell's smug languor told him much, and heat built in him. "Damn you, Hackwell. You knew."

The boots came down and clomped on the floor. "Knew what?"

Virgil swiped a hand through his hair. "I've intruded on your hospitality too long."

He hurried up the stairs, and at the door of his bedchamber paused. The door at the other end of the corridor was closed up tight.

He must see those girls again. If they were his, he would know, and he would stay. Bloody hell, this time there'd be no dismissing of anyone, and no running away.

CHAPTER SIX

THE NURSERY WAS QUIET WHEN VIRGIL WENT in. Hackwell's younger boy stretched in his bed, an arm thrown out. The older boy lay quietly, eyes shut. A third bed was empty.

"The girls aren't here."

Virgil looked into the bright blue eyes of the older boy who'd been after all, shamming.

"Their mama took them away."

Alarm sparked in him, and more anger, and he blinked, trying to clear his head. He'd heard no bustling of a carriage, had he? Blast it, he'd had far too much to drink.

"To where?" he asked.

"I don't know."

He scowled at the boy.

"To her bedchamber."

That whisper came from behind him, and he turned to see the maid he'd met on the staircase the first night.

"Now, Thomas, you're to close your mouth and go to sleep. Dee 'ad the sniffles and a tiny cough, milord, and Mrs. Dawes was worried. Besides that, these two keep waking up our girls."

Thomas protested. Virgil left them squabbling, and found his way down the stairs and corridor to the door across from his.

The latch gave way. She hadn't locked it.

He closed the door softly and paused inside. A lamp burned low upon the mantel, but he could see this room was as fine as his own, far finer than the servant's chamber Ameline had been allotted at his family's home so many years ago. A sofa sat in front of the fire, and a tester bed had rich hangings pulled about it. He went over and drew one back so the light from the lamp cast over the sleepers.

Emma and Dulciana lay in the center of the bed, covers drawn up, their mother curled around them.

Heat unfurled in him. Longing it was, naught to do with desire, not really. In the weeks they'd been lovers they'd never managed a whole night together, bundled up in such innocent intimacy. He watched for long moments, watched the little chests rise, and heard the rasping sound of congestion.

There was nothing so trivial as a simple cold. A simple cold had crept into something larger and killed his sister. He left the bed curtains open and went to the grate, stripping his coats and quietly feeding more coal. Then he drew off his boots and returned to the bed, stretching out on top of the covers and adding the warmth of his body. For the sake of the girls.

His girls.

A gentle snoring permeated Ameline's sleep. She snuggled deeper in the bedding, toasty warm, until she remembered Dulciana's cold. Her little girl wouldn't snore this loudly unless she was very ill.

She opened her eyes. The bed curtains had been pushed open, and though it must still be full dark outside, the room seemed brighter, and warmer.

Ameline raised herself upon her elbow and— *Virgil*.

Her heart pounded against her ribs. Virgil was in her *bed*. He'd seen the girls. The not so gentle snoring had been his.

Had been, because he now had one eye open, watching her.

He lay on top of the counterpane curled around Emma's other side, coatless, his shirt flopping around his neck.

"What are you doing?" she breathed. "How dare you?"

He must leave. What if Lady Hackwell found him here? She might lose her position at Longview. She might lose everything she'd built in the last three years. Oh, Lady Hackwell might understand, might not blame her—but what if she too accused her of being a seductress?

The Marquess of Wallenford wouldn't marry her to save her reputation—why should he, since she'd already borne his bastards? And why would she want that anyway? She'd have to give up the work she loved. She'd lose the freedom she'd built.

"I could say the same to you, Ameline."

The low rumble of his voice tried to worm its way through her resolve.

"Get out," she whispered.

"I won't."

Her heart thumped more wildly. "Then we'll leave." She tossed back the covers, then remembered she was in no more than a thin nightrail, and pulled them up again.

This was *her* bed. "You must go, Virgil."

"I won't."

"What if Lady Hackwell learns you were here? She is my *employer*. I work at her home for children. I need this living to support my daughters."

"My daughters."

Panic laced its way through her, as it had the day his brother had sacked her.

Virgil had discovered his daughters. She needed to leave without delay. She needed to take the girls and go home, where they'd be safe.

She squeezed a handful of bedding and took a deep breath. She'd found her way before, and she'd find her way now, even if they had to climb aboard another market cart like the day she'd left Willowbrook. Slipping from the covers, she collected her robe and went to feed the fire, needing practical activity to calm herself.

Thankfully, the girls still slept. Her children. Not his children. Never his. Except, that when Dee opened her eyes, he'd know she was his.

Her heart thudded. Or perhaps, he'd seen her already.

"Let me do that." Virgil nudged her aside, his voice tense. "Go and ring for some tea."

"I will *not*. It's the middle of the night. The servants are sleeping."

"Then sit." He cast the terse words over his shoulder.

She stomped about barefoot, fuming. She'd got him away from her bed—perhaps she could persuade him to move the conversation to a downstairs parlour.

His muscles stretched and bunched under his shirt and… his trousers. She pulled her robe tighter and averted her eyes, glancing back at the bed.

They were all right, for tonight. Tomorrow they must leave. Oh, but the girls would miss the party promised them.

Her stomach twisted. And Virgil would only follow her wherever she went. She might as well accept it—there'd be no outrunning this discussion.

She sat and scooted into the corner of the sofa. Virgil plopped down near her, and his heat swamped her. Drat the man, he still had this effect upon her.

She wrapped her arms across her chest and conjured the memory of her interview with his brother. There'd been much talk of *her* conduct, nothing about Virgil's, and plenty of discussion of how Virgil truly felt about her. Virgil had dallied, and he was done, and she should take the marquess's proffered banknote and handle any problem that arose.

At the memory, resentment roused, her reliable antidote to attacks of fancy. She'd left Willowbrook finally seeing the truth—she'd been seduced, used, and lied to. She'd left promising herself her child would never know his or her father.

She'd pulled up that memory when Virgil's name appeared on the list of the wounded at Waterloo. Every time she felt tempted to wonder if she'd been mistaken, she reminisced.

If he tried to take her girls...Oh God, she must find a way to forge the marriage lines with Mr. Dawes. Mrs. Crawford would know someone to help her. Or Lady Hackwell. In the eyes of the law, Dawes would be their father.

She squeezed her eyes shut against the weight of yet more betrayal, all around—Virgil's, hers, even Lady Hackwell's. Surely the Hackwells had put her in this predicament. Lady Hackwell had somehow pieced together the story of the young widowed mother who'd once worked for Lady Wallenford and the Waterloo hero. She might be Lady Hackwell's friend, but Wallenford and Hackwell were close, and everyone outranked a mere midwife.

"I walked into the Hackwells' drawing room tonight and discovered I'm the father of twins. I want to hear about my daughters."

Anger spiked in her, and she planted her feet upon the Axminster carpet and stiffened her back. "I assure you, they are not *your* daughters."

He opened his mouth, but she held up a hand.

"They are not yours. You renounced them."

His eyes darkened. "I did no such thing."

"Soon after you traveled up to London. You sent a letter to your brother, telling him that if I claimed anything...untoward, you would deny it." She swallowed hard and caught her breath. "You told him that I was destined to be a light-skirt. That I had tried to take advantage of your grieving."

"I wrote no such letter," he said calmly.

"Yes you did. He waved it in my face."

He turned upon the seat, cocked a knee against her leg, and stretched his arm along the sofa back. "And did he let you read this letter?"

"No."

"No. Because he was lying, Ameline."

Her throat tightened. For months she'd hoped Virgil's brother was lying, months while her belly had stretched and her ankles swelled, and she'd found herself begging a bed at Mrs. Crawford's home, praying for Virgil to ride up in the Wallenford coach and rescue her, wondering who would raise her child if she died.

She tried to move away but he touched her arm and sent tingling warmth through her.

"I sent him letters," he said, "reporting on the situation with Bonaparte, but I knew better than to mention you. I did, however, receive your note dismissing me."

Warm tears pressed against the back of her eyes. "Dismissing you? As we agreed, I sent a letter to you shortly after you left for London..." She rubbed her eyes. "Never mind." It had been star-crossed from the start and she'd best leave the past in the past.

He turned her chin and held her gaze, biting his lip, and finally speaking. "The letter casting me off arrived in my camp in Belgium, enclosed within one from my brother, and it was definitely dismissive."

The firm jaw, the full lips, oh, how she remembered. A newish thin scar traced his cheek, under his bristling stubble, and she could tell he didn't laugh so much anymore.

"Damn you, Virgil, I did send you a letter but not that one. I braved all of the proper world to send you, a single gentleman, a letter at Wallenford House, and then your brother called me in and told me your answer."

"A letter telling me you were with child?"

"I did not say it, no."

"But someone would have guessed. Someone who perhaps had once spotted us together."

He released her and leaned back, and his shirt gaped around a starburst scar, corded and jagged right above his heart.

She gasped and reached to touch it, but he clasped her hand and pushed it away.

"Waterloo?" she whispered. "I'd heard you were wounded, but—"

"I survived," he said in a tight voice.

Her lungs squeezed and her heart quickened. Had he? If so, it was just barely. He'd been stabbed or speared, or shot, and somehow, *somehow*, his great heart had carried on. This had been no minor wound. Virgil had suffered terribly.

"I want to see." She pushed his hand away and grasped his collar. He grabbed for her hand, but she dodged him and ripped the fine cotton, rending the shirt down the front.

"*Ameline—*"

"You have a trunk full of shirts. I want to see." She knelt before him on the sofa, yanked the shirt down his arms, and studied his chest. Small cuts marked his side and his belly, but the mottled scar was the worst. It would have taken months to fully heal a wound like this from the inside out. He should have died.

Her vision blurred so she couldn't see. But her hands, trained to examine a babe in the womb, they could see. She flattened her palms and set a course over the ridges knots, and hard ripples.

He surely had almost died. A world without Virgil, without his laughter, and his generally kind heart. He'd used her, true, as men did. It was in a man's animal nature, wasn't it? And she'd used him also, hadn't she? Both of them grieving over his sister's death, and comforting each other. And she was left with her girls, and things had turned out all right, hadn't they?

Her hands cupped his shoulders and slipped over to his back. No scars there that she could feel. The ball, or saber, or...what else did men use to kill each other?...had not gone clean through. It had merely dredged a hole in his front and wreaked havoc inside him.

And nearly killed him.

She'd always pictured a wounded Virgil, binding up a minor slash and heading off to the Continent to charm actresses and diplomats' wives, maybe taking a wife there himself, and bringing her back to breed pretty, cheerful children. Virgil, rich, content and happy.

How she'd wallowed in that vision.

The feel of the scarred skin melted away her resentment. Let him have that happy life with his marchioness and heirs. And perhaps, on a rare occasion, he could come down to Longview and visit his twins.

"Ameline." Virgil's breath touched her cheek.

Large hands cupped both of her hips.

Warmth spurted through her. Too late, she realized her error. She'd got too close again.

She pulled the sides of his shirt up, her gaze sliding over the rip and...

Right. He was fully erect. Of course he was.

Hot need shrieked inside her, and she battered it down and found her breath. "I apologize. My infernal curiosity." She patted his shoulders and eased away.

His eyes had gone dark and feral, his lips parted like a hungry man ready to chomp down on a long-awaited meal. Inside, she melted more.

She took in a great breath. She must keep him talking. "How did the wound happen?" she asked.

His eyes shuttered and he yanked her hard against him, smashing his lips to hers.

"*No.*"

He swallowed her protest, turning it into a moan.

Oh, and he tasted like brandy. His hand fanned over her bottom, pressing her closer. Like a man starving, his mouth demanded, and she opened for him.

Just one kiss. She quivered and snaked a hand round his neck. It had been so long, such sweetness to be kissed by Virgil. His tongue twined with hers, and his hands pressed her closer, her breasts against hard, bare skin.

Cold air touched her leg, and his hand slid along it, bringing her nightrail up.

No. She pulled away and sucked in great mouthfuls of air, and his lips moved to her neck, sending a shiver through her.

"Ameline," he whispered. "How I missed you, Ameline."

She blinked back tears. How she'd missed him, his kisses, his touch, his laughter.

She squeezed her eyes shut and thought of Virgil's brother. *Destined to be a light-skirt.* Virgil's hand on her leg moved higher, his lips lower to the tip of her breast, and she swallowed a laugh that bubbled up hysterically. With Virgil, she *was* a light-skirt.

Except now she had children to think about. "Stop." She wriggled, trying to pull away, and he tugged her closer. Her warm center touched the hard length of his shaft and she froze.

Pleasure pulsed in her. She wanted him. She wanted this. Just one night with the only man she'd ever loved, and…

She scooted away, and braced one hand on the twisted skin of his scar.

Virgil looked up, eyes dazed.

CHAPTER SEVEN

SHE'D GONE STIFF ON HIM.

Virgil caught his breath and tried to focus. The supple skin beneath his hand and the blood pounding through his cock made it hard. Made everything hard.

"I won't do it," she said.

Everything about her, tousled hair, swollen lips, frantic breaths, said she would. She needed a tumble as much as he did. He stroked a thumb along her thigh.

"No, Virgil."

"Dudududu." A stuttering, high-pitched moan came from the bed, and his hand froze.

He could see the hard pulsing of blood in Ameline's neck.

"The girls," she said, tugging away.

The girls. Of course. He'd been about to tup their mother with them in the nearby bed.

"It's Em," she said. "Let me off you. I don't want to wake them."

She lifted her hand from his chest, taking her warmth with her.

"Go to bed, Virgil."

Her whisper was as shaky as his breath. She was not unaffected, his Ameline, and not unwilling, either, no matter what she claimed. What they had between them hadn't died. She still wanted him, as much as he wanted her.

While she glared, he undid his cuffs, whipped the remains of his shirt over his head, and followed her to the bed.

She leaned over to feel heads and tuck blankets, her plump bottom rising before him.

"Still sleeping?" he whispered.

"Shhh."

One child frowned in her sleep, and the other twitched with a dream.

Which time had he planted those seeds? Was it one of the times in the orchard, or in the music room, or the time in the Wallenford coach? His cock ached thinking about it.

She moved back to the fireplace and he went also, happy to follow her anywhere.

"Dududubu," Emma moaned again.

Ameline warmed her hands. "For God's sake, Virgil, put on your coat."

She was averting her eyes from his nakedness. He inched closer and bent down to her ear. "I'm not cold. Why 'Dududubu'?" he whispered.

"It's what she used to call Dee. I don't know what the dream is."

"Not 'Dada' as in your Mr. Dawes?"

She bit down on her lip. "Go to bed, Virgil."

They weren't done yet, nor did he want to wake the girls. They should be in the nursery. He could carry them there. "Let me take them—"

"No." Ameline turned on him, eyes flashing, hands clenched in front of her, panicked.

He touched her shoulders. "Only upstairs to their bed." He smoothed his hands over the scratchy wool of her dressing gown. "Then we can talk in private. You can scream and throw things if you wish."

Her jaw firmed. "You'll not take my children anywhere."

"All right, Ameline. I won't take them anywhere." *Tonight.*

She shook her head. "You should return to your own bedchamber. We can talk...another time."

Bugger that. He wasn't waiting another minute. "No. We have to talk now."

"We'll wake them."

"We'll whisper."

A shiver went through her, and he leaned closer. She was unsettled, but not afraid.

"Come along," he said. "You're tired, but I can't let you get away from me again."

"You're the one who left, Virgil."

"And you were supposed to...oh, I know, my despicable brother sent you away, and my mother did nothing to help you. But I had Baker looking for you and finding nothing, not even a trail of bread crumbs."

She lowered herself to the edge of the cushion and he grabbed the coat he'd shed earlier and wrapped it around her.

"For heaven's sake, you wear it," she said, looking away from his bare chest, and the damn scar.

Well, he'd earned that mangled mess honestly, though he'd always counted it as a mark of his failure, not heroism. He'd wanted to die in that bloody, muddy field. "I'm not cold. Or...is the scar too ugly for you?"

Her eyes flashed, her mouth firmed. "Of course not. I not only deliver babies, I tend to wounds in the villages around Longview."

"Then keep the coat." He sat next to her.

She leaned forward and braced herself on the toes of her sweetly-arched feet. When she caught him staring, she scooted back and tucked them under her.

He reached for a foot, tugged it out, and propped it across his lap.

"What are you doing?" she asked, breathless.

"You're cold. I'm warming you."

He swept his palm across the bottom of her foot. Another tremble went through her and her eyes narrowed on him. "No, Virgil." She tried to yank her foot away but he held onto her ankle.

"We have two chaperones." He began chafing her sole with his hands. "You're very cold." And the way her eyes were darkening, very responsive.

"This is—"

He hit a ticklish spot, and she squeaked.

"I told you, I have a position to consider. You must stop."

He pressed the pad of his thumb into her foot. She jumped, and his cock came to life again.

In their few times together, he'd never made love to her feet.

She tried again to jerk away. "You must stop. The reputation of Longview...the reputation of staff must be impeccable. The children's futures, the patronesses..." She inhaled sharply and her eyes widened.

He'd found a new spot near her toes, and she gripped the cushions.

"Please stop. You *must* stop. My reputation...It's a good position, and I'm only able to..." She took in a sharp breath. "As a, a respectable widow."

His hand stilled. "Of Mr. Dawes?"

"Yes."

A bilious spurt of jealousy settled sourly in his stomach.

"And I suppose he is listed as the girls' father in the baptismal register?"

"Yes."

An ache built within him. He released her foot and watched it disappear under garments. "And he was killed at Waterloo?"

She lifted her shoulder and nodded.

Memories of smoke, and shouting, and blinding explosions clouded him. He eased in a breath. "And what do you tell everyone he did before?"

"He was, er, employed. It must be this way. You're a great lord now. I didn't send you a note casting you off, but I should have. It was wise of your mother or brother to write whatever they sent you. And you must forget me. Cast me aside. Find a pretty young heiress. And my daughters—"

"They're my daughters too, Ameline. You can't hide that fact."

She choked in a breath and batted her eyes, and his heart lifted. She was his, she just hadn't accepted it yet.

"Thank you for giving them my sister's names."

She nodded and dipped her head, and he waited while she composed herself.

"I couldn't have her be another forgotten girl. Do not worry about Dulciana and Emma. They have good lives, and I'll make them into true ladies, no matter what role they must play in life."

"Each of my daughters will play a lady's role."

"You'll marry and have many daughters, my lord. You can name them all Lady Dulciana or Lady Emma if your wife does not fight you on it. This Dulciana and Emma, you must forsake."

Oh no, he wouldn't. "I cannot." He pulled out her other foot and went to work on it.

"Stop that, Virgil." She squeaked and blushed when he hit a ticklish spot. "And why not? It was an easy enough thing for your father to lock his own child away and forget her." She leaned back and huffed. "Oh, blast you, but that feels good. But you must walk away from the girls, Wallenford. I make no claims on you."

"The children's claims are the issue we are discussing tonight."

Her lips contorted, and he wanted to fling her down on the sofa and cry out—*And yours. Always yours. It's about you. It's always been about you.*

He patted her foot, released it, and moved closer. "I will take care of them. And you, Ameline."

Her gaze searched his, and even as she shook her head, his heart filled—she wanted to believe.

"There is no need. Your brother was right to keep us apart, Virgil. Perhaps he knew then he was dying, and you would inherit. Perhaps—"

"Shhh." He pressed a finger to her lips. "He was an insufferable ass, as was my father. And I wish one of them was still alive to wear the yoke of this title. I never wanted it."

"Is that why you stayed away so long?"

"No, at least not entirely."

"You were on the king's business?"

"I was, but I could have thrown that aside and come home. I stayed gone because I thought the woman I loved didn't want me."

She frowned, looking so utterly puzzled he wanted to shake her, and then her gaze narrowed and her mouth firmed.

"Caroline?" she asked.

Caroline?

What a fool he'd been, staying away because he'd lost Ameline, because he didn't want his mother pushing a bride on him, especially not one like Caroline, who'd broken with him and taken up his brother, and then more likely delayed that marriage when she'd discovered he was sick. After all, the widowed marchioness could not legally marry her late husband's brother.

Ameline's mouth had locked into a belligerent frown and he swallowed a smile. She knew he'd long since moved past his childhood *tendre* for Caroline. She knew he didn't care about the woman who became his brother's fiancée. She was merely prodding him for a reaction.

"Don't be a nodcock. I don't love Caroline. What did you say in that letter you sent to me at Wallenford House?"

She huffed, annoyed. Good.

"I asked you for news of Bonaparte. I sent news of your grandmother. Is she still alive?"

He shook his head.

"Oh. My condolences." She took in a deep breath. "I also wrote to you that Dulciana's daffodils had bloomed."

If you have need, write to me, he'd told her, and that was the code they'd agreed upon. How could his brother have known?

"Had they?"

"No." She shook her head. "Just after you left, your mother had the gardener dig them up and plant roses."

An ache started behind his eyes and he rubbed at it. Dulcie had loved her daffodils. "In any case, the letter never reached me. Did my brother at least give you any money, Ameline? Did he pay you to go away?"

She inhaled sharply and stood. "Pay me? You mean, did I take money to leave?"

"Yes." He shook his head. "Dammit, I mean no." He reached for her hand, but she pulled away.

"This is getting us nowhere."

A whimpering came from the bed. One of the girls sat up, rubbed her eyes, and began to cry.

He headed for the bed, but Ameline flung his coats at him, took his arm and whisked him to the door.

He dug in his heels—his stocking-clad heels.

The other girl sat up and joined in with a wail that tugged at his heart.

"Now look what you've done," Ameline said. "We'll wake the whole household."

"I'll help—"

"Leave." Her eyes flashed at him, her hair in such wild disarray he wanted to sink his hands into it and kiss her one more time and maybe never stop. That would shock the girls out of their crying.

She flattened a palm against his chest, but her attention was all directed toward the bed where his daughters were vying for her attention.

So this was fatherhood. He set a finger under her chin and she turned his way, in such a wild mix of anger and concern and frustration he wanted—he needed—to stay. She needed him.

But his being here added one more aggravation to the mix, one that she wasn't ready for. "All right. We'll talk tomorrow. We're not finished yet, Ameline."

"Oh, we're finished."

"May I get my boots?"

Her gaze traveled down him and, moments later, she thrust his boots at him. "Here. Now leave."

"I will. Good night."

At the bed, a body was lowering itself down by the sheets, like a sailor going over the side on a line. He swallowed a chuckle and dropped a quick kiss on Ameline's cheek. "Tomorrow, then. I love you, Ameline."

Moments later he sat in his banyan by the dwindling coals in his own chamber, arguing with himself about going back down the corridor to her chamber.

He'd found her, and he'd talked to her. He'd made progress—frustrating, annoying, torturous progress. He'd talk her around.

And by God, he wanted her, and whether Ameline would admit it or not, she was ready to take him back as a lover.

He gripped the arms of his chair. If the girls hadn't been there tonight...well, it wouldn't take much more than one night in that bed to convince her to hang up her midwife's smock and put on a coronet. Blast it, he didn't want to live this life without her.

The noise down the corridor diminished, but even as his girls were quietening, elsewhere another child had taken up the call of the wild.

He laughed. Since Waterloo, he'd never been able to sleep much. Perhaps he *was* made for fatherhood.

And by God, he'd be a good father to his girls. Their girls.

*****

Virgil woke the next morning with a throbbing head, having finally slept for a bit. He dressed quickly and peeked in her room.

His hair prickled. The room was empty and tidied, with no personal items around. Nor could he see a travel case.

Had there been one the night before? He hadn't stopped to look at anything more than the girls and Ameline in her night clothes.

He hurried down the stairs and found her bundling them out of the front door to a waiting carriage. A squat trunk was strapped on, and a servant handed in a food hamper, big enough for a trip to Scotland.

Virgil flew out the door and signaled the coachman. "Hold up," he yelled.

He threw himself onto the rear facing seat and found himself confronted by three frowning females.

CHAPTER EIGHT

AMELINE'S HEART POUNDED AS SHE WRAPPED an arm around each girl.

They were both cross, as was she from their interrupted sleep. After Virgil had departed, she'd got the girls back down, but her feet—and other parts of her—had been far too aroused for slumber.

"Lord Wallenford," she said.

"Running away?" He straightened his coats with those strong, broad hands and then raked them through his dark hair. He had the clean fingernails of a gentleman, and of course, he'd run after her without gloves or a hat.

"Certainly not."

Though she *had* contemplated moving lodgings and keeping her girls out of Virgil's sight.

A sour taste rose into her mouth. She could run, but Virgil was their father, and some day, they would want the truth. It all made her head hurt.

"You're leaving with a travel trunk and a large basket of food. Why do I not believe you?"

Why did the aristocracy think the world revolved around them?

"The trunk is filled with infant clothing for poor mothers, made by the girls at Longview. The food basket is a gift for a dear friend. And we'll come back because Lady Hackwell is preparing a birthday party when we return from our call. Now go back inside before you freeze."

"I am a man. I won't freeze on a short trip to...Sussex, isn't that where you reside?"

She rolled her eyes, opened the door, and waved to the footman. "Please go and get Lord Wallenford's hat, gloves and overcoat. We will wait."

"How are your sniffles, Dulciana?" he asked. "Should you be going out in the cold?"

Dee slid her a sideways glance. She'd been bright-eyed that morning, with no trace of a cough or fever.

"I believe she is well."

"I ate my bekfast," Dee said.

The mention of breakfast sent an ominous growl through the coach—Virgil's stomach. Dee giggled and Em joined in.

"Well, lucky for you, little misses," he said. "Is there aught in that basket I can nibble on while we wait?"

"You can go in and load a plate from the sideboard," Ameline said, "and we'll be on our way."

"Oh, now I'm getting more and more curious about this expedition. Where are we going, Mrs. Dawes?"

A footman opened the door and passed in Virgil's hat, gloves, and overcoat. He pulled the tight gloves over his strong hands, but set the hat on the seat next to him and arranged the overcoat over her and the girls.

Ameline's face heated and she hid a shiver. He scarce had to lean forward in the cramped coach, his knees knocking against hers, his long arms reaching clear to the squabs behind them.

He rapped, and the coach pulled out.

"Where are we going?" he asked again.

"We are paying a visit to an old friend."

"Who is this old friend?"

"My granny," Dee called from the bundle of wool.

"My granny, too," Em growled.

Virgil sent Ameline a sharp look.

He would call her a liar again. She'd told him she was an orphan, and it was true. Her parents' parents were gone, and all of their siblings. There were cousins—distant ones, who she'd never met.

She sighed. "An honorary granny. Mrs. Crawford is the midwife who gave me shelter, brought these two into the world, and taught me everything I know about midwifery."

"We're visiting a midwife?" he drawled. "On Christmas morning?"

There was enough irony in his tone to make her stomach clench and send heat into her cheeks. Perhaps Virgil had succeeded his brother in both title and self-importance, and, God help her, probably character too. The next time he tried to rub one of her feet, she'd best remember he was a great lord now.

They'd turned out of the Hackwells' square but hadn't gone far. "I'll just tell the coachman to take you back," she said. "It won't delay us much."

He raised an eyebrow.

She lifted her chin and sat up straighter. "You don't want to come with us. You're far too high now for such a visit as this, though we're lucky, thanks to Lord Hackwell's kindness, to be traveling in such style. You know, the day I left your ancestral manor, I rode on the market cart out of Willowbrook to the village inn."

Dee shifted on the seat, dislodging her covers. Outside, in spite of the feast day, the streets teamed with walkers, merchants and carriages, and she wanted to see. Their coach lurched and Virgil grabbed for her. "Steady there, Dulciana. Come and climb on my knee, and you'll have a better view from such a great height."

Ameline watched him take first Dee, then Em onto his knees, and forced her own hands to unfist.

She'd sat on his lap long ago, in a coach much like this one, the last time they were together. Beads of sweat dampened her brow. Her cheeks must be blooming even more because Virgil grinned. He remembered also.

She squeezed her hands tight. She so wanted to plant a facer on him.

His smile slipped into a frown. "Go on with your story. What happened at the village inn?"

"I took a room. It was late. I *had* been given some money."

"By whom?"

"Your mother sent a maid with coins and notes. And your brother..." Her head pounded. Virgil's brother had given her a bank note. *You'll find a midwife in London to attend to your problem.* "The next day I took a top seat on the coach. I was ill, as sometimes happens at that stage of..." She glanced at Dee, who had her nose pressed to the window, Virgil's strong hand spanning her waist, steadying her. "At that stage. To make a long story short, at the next town, I was introduced to a woman—a midwife, who was Mrs. Crawford's good friend. I came up to London and apprenticed with Mrs. Crawford. Eventually, through her, I came to know Miss Harris—who became Lady Hackwell."

"I see," he said flatly.

He didn't see. He didn't know anything. She didn't tell him about dodging the gropes of the men on the coach, or pawning her mother's necklace, or making do with the one extra dress she had shoved into her travel bag.

And she couldn't talk about any of that in front of the girls. "Where did *you* go?" she asked.

"Waterloo, of course. And then I spent several months in a hospital in Belgium, with Mother threatening to come over as soon as my brother recovered from his illness. And then word came of his demise, and that was the end of that. By then, I was in Vienna."

How nice for him. Instead of coming back and taking up the responsibilities of a great lord and landowner, he'd swanned about Europe.

After his time in the hospital, she chided herself. It didn't take a medical person to see that the wound had not been *nice*. The wound should have killed him.

"Was it a ball, or a saber?" she asked.

"A ball they say, though devil if I knew anything of it at the time."

"You're lucky to be alive."

He huffed, pulled a sliding Em higher, and smiled. "I am now."

She struggled for breath—*he'd just threatened to take her daughters.*

He was using them to bully her. All the kisses and talk the previous night had meant nothing, just a lord trying to worm his way into a woman's bed, and oh, she'd been tempted. After he left her chamber, she'd had hours of battling with her common sense, and her common sense had won. Virgil might want her in his bed, but he wouldn't marry her, and in spite of his denials, he was very likely to take the easiest path and simply acquiesce to his mother's plans for him.

She unclenched her hands.

"What of Caroline's feelings?" she asked. "In spite of your denials, I hear I am to wish you both happy."

His gaze shot up and his jaw firmed, but the coach stopped, and before he could answer and call her a nodcock again, the step was dropped and the door opened, and Brenda Crawford was reaching up to greet the girls.

"Come in, come in." Mrs. Crawford took each girl by the hand. "How you've grown, little poppins. Happy Christmas to all."

Ameline tried to hurry ahead, but Virgil's hand touched her elbow.

They walked in as a couple, and she saw his gaze inspect the worn hall and beyond, into the packed drawing room.

Furniture and children cluttered the narrow house squeezed into a back street not far from Mayfair. Three years earlier, Ameline had looked up with trepidation at the tall facade, but she'd slipped in as easily as a book on a generous shelf, taking the bed Mrs. Crawford opened now and again to the gentlewomen with hard cases who had nowhere else to turn.

They handed over the food basket, shed coats, and the girls ran off to the drawing room shrieking along with the children already gathered there. Mrs. Crawford cleared her throat. "Dear Ameline," she said. "You look well. And greetings, sir. I'm Brenda Crawford."

Ameline roused herself. "Mrs. Crawford, this is—"

"Virgil Radcliffe." He bowed.

Mrs. Crawford bowed back. "The knees won't work for a curtsy, milord."

Virgil sighed, a grin forming. "Caught out."

The older lady smiled. "It's in the eyes. Spitting image of Dee's, are they not, Ameline?"

Ameline's insides turned over, but thankfully the noise in the drawing room would drown out this discussion. "The girls haven't been told."

Mrs. Crawford eyed Virgil up and down. "You'll do right by your children?"

"I will."

"Full of promises, men are." Her gaze flitted to Ameline and back. "And what about our Ameline?"

"I mean to take care of her also."

Mrs. Crawford harrumphed.

"Honorably." One side of his mouth went up in a lopsided grin. "Though I should like to have that discussion with her first. Or perhaps I should ask your permission?"

"Ameline is her own woman," Mrs. Crawford said.

"And Ameline is standing right here. I have a profession, and I'm quite able to take care of myself. I don't need your help, my lord."

"Everyone needs help sometimes," Mrs. Crawford said. "I had Mr. Crawford as a helpmate for so many years, God rest his soul. And he gave me a great deal of experience with bringing babes into the world." She laughed. "It's a blessing to have a strong shoulder to rest on when things go awry, and his lordship here seems to have broad ones."

Ameline shook her head.

"Well, and perhaps his pockets are deep enough to throw a few pence toward someone who does need help?"

"How is Miss Smith?" Ameline asked.

Mrs. Crawford frowned.

"Miss Smith?" Virgil asked.

"I have a young woman upstairs." She took Ameline's arm. "First you'll have tea, and then you may examine her. Her time will be very soon. I've sent a note round to Mr. Baxter to have his bag ready."

Ameline stopped. "Why?" Calling in an accoucheur was the last resort. She let out a breath. "Will you need him?"

"I believe so. I should like your opinion after you examine her. You'll help with the birth?"

"Of course, as we agreed. You must send for me at Lady Hackwell's."

"So you'll stay a while longer?" Virgil asked.

Blast it. She'd forgotten about him hovering nearby.

A girl of about ten came to the drawing room door. "There are nuts, and sweetmeats, and lemon tarts in the basket, Granny," she said.

Mrs. Crawford chuckled. "Will you join our merry bunch, my lord?"

"I most certainly will." He offered an arm to the older lady. "I missed my breakfast, you know."

An hour later, Ameline left the children playing, and Virgil talking with Mrs. Crawford's grown daughters and sons, and popped into a small bedchamber under the eaves.

The attending maid curtsied, and the woman in the bed turned a wan smile on Ameline and greeted her.

Ameline's heart sank. The starving woman who'd shown up at Longview months earlier had blown up so, she could hardly see the pretty young lady inside.

She forced a smile. "I've brought some tea and cakes from the party downstairs. Aggie, run along and I'll sit with Miss Smith for a bit. Now," she lifted the plate, "what shall it be? Gingerbread or lemon tart?"

The maid scuttled out and Miss Smith poked at the selection of food. "Are you here to help deliver my baby? Mrs. Crawford said you were in town for Lady Hackwell's lying in. Is she well?"

"Quite well, as is the babe. As will you be. I'll certainly help Mrs. Crawford if she needs me. Though I think her back is almost recovered and she may be able to manage this one on her own."

Miss Smith shook her head. "She's called in a man. He came to examine me last week." Her mouth twisted up. "I'm going to die, aren't I?" she whispered.

Ameline raised her up, plumped a pillow and frowned at her. "Not if Mrs. Crawford and I can help it."

"Please, will you see to my baby? Make sure it lives and see that it's taken care of. Will you do that, Mrs. Dawes?"

"She will," said a masculine voice.

Ameline closed her eyes and took in a deep breath, even as she heard Virgil's footsteps crossing the spare space.

Miss Smith's hands flew up and smoothed her cap.

A visit by a handsome lord would discompose any woman. "Virgil—"

"So this is the room." He bowed to Miss Smith. "My apologies, miss. I'm Virgil Radcliffe. I wanted to see the room where my girls were born."

Miss Smith raised up on an elbow, eyes searching his face, cheeks flaming. "You're the father of Mrs. Dawes's girls?" She huffed, her breathing clearly labored.

If merely sitting up in bed exhausted her, how would they get her through the exertion of childbirth?

Miss Smith turned her gaze on Ameline. "There was no Mr. Dawes?"

She shook her head. "Like you, I had no marriage certificate to give me access to the Lying-in Hospital."

Miss Smith glared at Virgil. "You ran off too. You left her."

"No." He and Ameline spoke as one.

Her heart beat faster. Virgil had turned the full force of his attention upon her, a look of wonder in his eyes.

Well, it was true. "It was more complicated than that," Ameline said. "There were...circumstances, and others keeping us apart."

Virgil took her hand and his eyes softened. "Thank you, Ameline. I'm glad you see that."

"Like Romeo and Juliet?" Miss Smith grimaced.

"Are you in pain, my dear?" Ameline pulled her hand loose and rested it on the young woman's cheek.

"A bit."

"Let me find Aggie's cool cloth," she pulled a wet flannel from a basin, "and then I'll examine you. Will you step out, Virgil?"

"Of course." He reached for Miss Smith's hand. "Do not worry, Miss Smith. Whatever happens, Ameline and I will see you and your child well taken care of."

The blue eyes widened and the young woman nodded, and Virgil slipped out.

Ameline took the hand and studied it. Virgil's brief touch had left imprints in the puffy skin. She'd never seen edema this severe.

"He's very handsome," Miss Smith said. "And he seems...kind. Will you marry then, Mrs. Dawes?"

She shook her head and peeled back the covers. "No. Let's have a look at this babe then."

"Why ever not....oh. Oh, I see. He's married."

"No. Virgil is not married. He's titled. He's a marquess, and I'm a midwife. Roll on your side now, will you?"

She saw the first flash of tears and squeezed her lips together. Miss Smith was gentry stock also, caught, much like herself, in a trap of her own romantic notions. She had managed to spring out of those jaws and land on her feet. Useful work was a good balm for any wound. God willing, Miss Smith would find some purpose also.

"Mine was a squire's son. A neighbor," Miss Smith said in a strained voice. "Since married."

"We can help you to seek a settlement. He should have to pay."

"I'll think about it."

Think quickly. Mrs. Crawford was right—the babe had turned in the womb, and Miss Smith's time would be soon—and, perhaps, as Mrs. Crawford had said, perilous.

She truly wasn't such an experienced midwife. She'd never seen the effects of toxaemia—surely that's what this was—in a childbirth.

She forced a smile. "There now. Let's cover you. I'm happy to say you'll be holding your babe soon." She tucked the covers around her. "Shall we have another look at those cakes?"

Downstairs, Virgil found his way to the drawing room and looked in. Little bellies had been filled, and the tumult had quietened. His girls sprawled with Mrs. Dawes's grandchildren in a field of half-dressed dolls, stubby fingers yanking at miniature gowns and fastenings. He backed out and wandered down the corridor, and found Mrs. Crawford in a small sort of study, her cap tightly framing her round face.

"Well?" She looked up from her papers and a smile lit her eyes.

He'd guess she'd never been a handsome woman, yet her face, infused with good humor, had its own allure. Mrs. Crawford's beauty came from inside.

"Thank you for your kindness to Ameline and my girls." He thought of the young woman lying upstairs. "Was Ameline's childbirth hard?" *Did I almost lose her?*

"Ameline did well, but twins are always hard."

A familiar sadness washed over him. "I'm a twin."

"Ameline told me. Your sister came second and the delay and the difficulty injured her."

"Yes, I was the first." The spare. How fortunate he'd come first, else the spare would have been a blithering idiot, his father had said.

The words stirred bitterly inside him.

"It certainly wasn't your fault," Mrs. Crawford said.

"My mother blamed the midwife."

"And likely it wasn't the midwife's fault either. But Ameline told me your father chased her from the village. Our poor lass had to travel a day's journey to seek help. We do our best, but sometimes we lose them."

"Has Ameline ever lost a mother or child?"

"No, mercifully not. She's studied hard, and she loves the work. I almost hesitated to ask for her help with Miss Smith, because I am sorry to say...well, we may need a miracle."

"The swelling?" he asked. "Isn't that part of every maternity?"

"Not to this extent. Do you believe in miracles, my lord?"

He swiped a hand across his face. "It's Christmas. And yes, I suppose I must. I've found Ameline and my children alive and well." And then there was Waterloo. Against the odds and his own desire for death, he'd survived those wounds. Hope rose in him. "It may take a miracle to persuade Ameline to marry me. And meanwhile, how can we save Miss Smith and her child?"

She shook her head. "The surgeon I've called in, Mr. Baxter, is a man keen to discover a remedy, as am I. Short of taking the child by a caesarian birth, which would almost surely kill the mother, we must see this through and pray. It is a hard thing."

It would be a hard thing for Ameline.

Mrs. Crawford stood, and Virgil rose with her.

"Is your mother still living, Lord Virgil?"

"She is."

"And has she blessed your marriage plans?"

He pressed his lips together.

"No, I see not. Ameline said your mother was not unkind. Perhaps you could win her over first and ease the way. I've seen many things over the years, Lord Virgil. It's a hard thing for a woman who's borne a titled man's bastards to take up as his wife." She patted his arm. "You must pardon my plain speaking, and do not frown so. I'm sure your powers of persuasion are up to the challenge."

He couldn't help but smile. "You leave me with hope." Scant hope. He would have to travel to Willowbrook if he were to win over his mother first, and then persuade Mother that Caroline really was unsuitable to be his bride.

And meanwhile, would Ameline disappear again?

The drive back from Mrs. Crawford's took longer, the traffic being snarled. Dulciana and Emma had been petted and played with, chased by

Mrs. Crawford's grandsons, and in turn had bedeviled the older midwife's cat.

When he took them on his lap, they fell instantly asleep.

Seated across from him, Ameline was either studying the floor or dozing. After the pleasant visit with the jolly Brenda Crawford, it was clear to Virgil—Ameline loved her work.

But as a marchioness she couldn't be mucking about delivering babies for farmers and laborers.

And in London, it was dangerous work indeed, for any man or woman. Mrs. Crawford kept a tidy home, but typhus, cholera, any number of ailments lurked in the rookeries and homes of the lower orders, and even in the charity hospitals. Perhaps especially in the charity hospitals. She might bring disease home to her children.

Their children. If she refused to marry him, it was an argument he could use to take the girls.

His stomach roiled. He knew he couldn't do that to Ameline.

Her gaze lifted and her lips pressed together.

"Your mother visited yesterday, did you know?" she asked.

CHAPTER NINE

THE WORDS JOLTED VIRGIL.

Blast it. Mother was supposed to be in the country, staying away from the temptations of London, squeezing her allowance a little more tightly. He was not a skinflint by any means, but he'd had to put limits on her spending. If she was rattling around London, running up bills at the modiste and ordering in mountains of coal, well—

"Caroline was with her." The words came out tense and raspy, as if saying the name made Ameline's throat hurt.

Hearing it certainly made his head hurt. And why the devil had Hackwell not told him about his mother's visit?

Perhaps the Hackwells didn't know. Perhaps Hackwell had been out, and his lady had been confined to her chamber, and Mother had stumbled in on Ameline.

But the girls—had Mother seen them? Would she notice the resemblance? Would she suspect they were his?

His heart pounded. His mother had dutifully followed Father's orders about her own daughter. He'd assumed she'd been complicit with his brother in sending Ameline away. She'd always been congenial with Ameline in private, when his father or brother was not around. But that didn't mean she wanted Ameline as a daughter-in-law.

And...he needed to win her over, as Mrs. Crawford had advised. He needed to make his mother an ally in winning Ameline's hand.

"Your mother is staying with Caroline's family."

That news, delivered so smugly, sent heat roaring through him. "And no one saw fit to inform me of this visit?"

She tilted her head and looked down her nose. "His lordship did not tell you? He was there, after all, he and Lady Hackwell and the rascally Thomas."

Emma stirred on his lap, but a quick glance told him she was still sleeping.

"But not them," Ameline whispered.

He let out a tight breath. Mother had not discovered his children. They might have a chance to speak before she leaked news of an engagement between the Marquess of Wallenford and Miss Caroline Jermyn to one of the scandal sheets. He might...he looked into two glaring dark eyes.

Ameline's gaze burned him. "Do you suppose Caroline will like having another woman's ch-children around?"

His heart did a flip. She was poking him again, and feeling the pain herself, her lips pressed so tightly he wanted to see about forcing them open. Except, he had two slumbering chaperones in his arms.

And bugger Caroline, how many times did he have to say it? He wasn't going to marry her. The woman he wanted—the woman he still wanted—was right here in front of him.

He smiled. "I get the occasional letter from Mother, but she didn't mention Caroline marrying a widower."

Ameline's lips contorted, her cheeks coloring brightly. "Let us have this clear between us, Virgil. Dee and Em will live with me."

"In a home for orphaned children?"

"We have our own cottage on the grounds."

"And when you're off delivering babies—"

"One of the older girls watches them."

He had to give her credit. She'd managed well, giving the girls a home and keeping her freedom to pursue work she loved. Back at Willowbrook, she'd managed to attend the occasional village party or family dinner, but mostly she'd spent her time in his sister's rooms. She wasn't a piece of London frippery. Persuading her to trade her quiet life and her work for a marchioness's burdens might be a hard bargain.

Though there were political advantages to being a marchioness, none that his mother had exerted, but then she'd been under the heavy thumb of his father and brother. Ameline was more imaginative than his mother. And the work of a midwife had pitfalls and burdens she hadn't encountered yet. Mrs. Crawford had said as much.

He thought of Miss Smith in her room under the eaves, but couldn't bring himself to mention her upcoming ordeal. He needed another argument.

He glanced out of the window and spotted a bedraggled woman, thin as a broomstick, bedeviling walkers with a handful of flowers. If Ameline worked in London, she might very well visit a woman like this, dirty, probably vermin-infested, and wracked with some disease or other.

"There is much needing to be done for these poor women," he said.

"I'm glad you see that. I intend to do what I can."

"And what if, Ameline, you bring an illness home from one of your patients?"

"It is a risk, more in London than in the countryside. But illness could strike anyone, at any time." She leaned forward. "I'm not giving up my work."

"You love it that much?"

"I do."

He sighed. "Have you had any, er, unsuccessful births? Have you lost a mother or child?"

She shook her head. "No. Of course I accept the possibility, but I've been very fortunate. And I keep up with the latest medical practices. Mrs. Crawford trained with Margaret Stephens, she who studied under Dr. Smellie and wrote the book about midwifery."

"You would not give it all up to have a husband and family of your own?"

You would not give it up for me?

A thin trickle of moisture traveled down his back while he watched her frowning and choosing her words.

"Mrs. Crawford has a husband and children, as did Mrs. Stephens. Though my plans regarding marriage are my affair."

His ears pricked. This was a wrinkle he hadn't thought of. "Have you someone in mind?"

She gave him a long look. "That would be my business."

"And the girls' well-being is my business. You may have seen fit to conceal them from me for more than three years, but now that I've found them, I'll see to their care."

Ameline huffed. "I did not conceal them. And you will not take them. And I'm sure your mother and Caroline, or whoever you marry, would have something to say about these two joining your household."

"Caroline will never have a say in anything." Nor would his mother have a say, nor would Ameline bring a stepfather in to care for his children. Be damned with that. "Are you planning to marry, Ameline?"

Her brows squeezed together and she let out a long breath. "No. And I did not conceal them from you, Virgil."

"I *did* try to find you."

She opened her mouth but before she could speak, the carriage stopped, and the girls came to life in his arms.

Outside, Ameline straightened the skirts of her gown. "Put them down, Virgil," she said.

Dee turned her sleepy head away and wrapped both arms around Virgil's neck, grabbing a fistful of hair, and sending a prickle of envy through Ameline.

Virgil endeared himself to all of the female sex, except possibly Caroline Jermyn. A shiver went through her, remembering the feel of his hair through her fingers. He'd seduced her with kindness, and friendship, and good humor. She wished he would do it again. She shook off the thought and climbed the steps.

"I'll just get you both up the steps, little ones, shall I?" he said.

At the landing he set both girls on their feet and lifted the knocker.

"Ameline."

His touch on her arm sent a sizzle through her.

"I *did* look for you. I sent Baker after you, even after I left for Belgium. I had to go, Ameline, as a matter of duty. And I only had Baker stop looking when I got the letter from you. Which I know now, you didn't send."

The letter his mother had sent. She looked past him, at the square, where rain had puddled to mud. It had rained at Waterloo, she'd heard, men and horses covered in mud, and blood, and cannon ash. She sighed. "And then you were wounded, and couldn't come back."

That one glimpse of his mended wound had made her heart seize. She wanted to see it again, wanted to lift up his shirt again and see all of him. And there was his limp, very slight, but not always mastered. They'd not had a chance to discuss that wound.

She turned back and the heat of his gaze all but melted her.

"I never forgot you," he said.

"Open up," Dee said. Both girls began to pound the door, but all Virgil's attention was on her.

And I still love you. She pressed her lips tight on the words.

"I tried to find you. I had Baker making inquiries all over England. May we talk later?" He squeezed her hand. "In private, after these two have gone to bed, which I think should probably be very soon."

Ameline sucked in a sharp breath. "Their birthday. Oh, I hope we have not delayed the party."

Both girls clutched at her skirts and began to whine.

A loud throat-clearing sent warmth to Ameline's cheeks. Alton held the door open. How much had he heard?

"They're waiting for you in the drawing room." He ushered them in, handing their outerwear to another servant.

A howl told her the boys were already arguing.

Dee shot off, but Virgil caught up and tossed her, tickling a laugh out of her, while Em clung to his leg, demanding a share of attention. Ameline hurried to catch up and entered the drawing room.

And her heart all but stopped.

Lady Wallenford and Caroline had joined the party again.

CHAPTER TEN

CAROLINE'S STARTLED LOOK WAS QUICKLY shuttered. Sitting across from Thomas at the small game table, Lady Wallenford smiled over Robby, who sat on her lap, a handful of cards in hand. When she glanced up, her face paled and the stark pleasure there convulsed through a range of emotions.

"Virgil." His mother choked out the word.

"There you are," Lady Hackwell said pleasantly. "And now we may begin the birthday celebration."

Hackwell stood. "Wallenford, I believe you know our two guests."

"Down," Dee said, wriggling.

"Very well, birthday girl." Virgil planted a kiss on Dee's brow, sending her into more giggles, and bent to kiss Em also. As soon as Dee's feet hit the ground both girls ran to the table. Lady

Wallenford's mouth dropped open and stayed that way.

Ameline's breath hitched, fatigue and worry catching up with her, memories flooding her.

"Miss Illington."

The marquess oozed contempt, sending a flurry of bile to her throat. She eased in a breath, quelling the nausea, and the screech of her nerves.

"I hear you've not been well," he said.

Her knees threatened to buckle and she glanced at the padded armchair positioned in front of his writing table.

"No," he said. "Do not be seated. You won't be here long." He waved a letter, the seal broken. "My brother has written to me, explaining how you took advantage of his grief. Shall I tell you what he said? That you are destined to be a light-skirt."

Everything rose in her—blood, heat, more bile. She clutched the chair back and struggled to breathe, the hard beat of her pulse obscuring the words—clipped, sharp, cutting—without blunting them.

He paused, grasped the corner of a paper, and handed it to her. "I suppose you thought that my brother would marry you, and that Mother and I would countenance such a connection. Take this and be done. You'll find a midwife in London to attend to you. Go and take care of any problems you have created, and do not bother Lord Virgil again. He can find himself a less expensive whore."

She fought for breath, fought to quell a rising nausea. Virgil slipped his hand around hers, enveloping that small part of her in his warmth and...strength.

She glanced up at him. He'd grown into a man, his own man, and would marry the woman of his own choice. Not her of course, but perhaps not Caroline either, and that sent a smug glee through her. She straightened and squeezed his hand. She could help him with this act of rebellion, and perhaps he wouldn't try to take her girls away from her to live with him.

"I am dutifully surprised, Mother. May I wish you a happy Christmas? And Miss Jermyn, my condolences on the loss of your beloved fiancé. You both must have been devastated when my brother died instead of me."

Caroline's mouth firmed in a straight line of neither pleasure nor pain. Lady Wallenford's attention ripped from the girls to Virgil, her face contorting.

She'd heard Virgil's words, but not understood, not immediately, and the dagger's blade pierced slowly.

Ameline's heart ached. Virgil had thrown down the gauntlet, letting everyone know he wouldn't be bullied, but perhaps his mother was the wrong adversary. Perhaps the bullies who'd caused so much pain, to his mother, his sister, and Ameline, were dead.

Bile rose in her. And he was taking up their role.

She squeezed his hand. "Virgil," she scolded, in a whisper.

"Why ever would you say that, Virgil?" Lady Wallenford's voice cracked on the words. She stood and gently set Robby aside. "I've missed you terribly these three-and-a-half years."

As she crossed the room, Ameline tried to drop his hand, but he held on. Lady Wallenford noticed and frowned.

"And here is Ameline," Virgil said.

His mother's mouth moved like she was sucking on something sour. "Miss Illington." She set her hands on Virgil's shoulders, and Ameline wrested her hand free.

"I'm so glad you're home." Lady Wallenford moved closer, smoothing her palms down his arms. "I've longed to have you home. It has been such a dreadful few years."

Virgil's jaw tightened. "Indeed."

"Welcome home, Virgil. We're so glad you've returned safely." Caroline turned a smile on her hostess. "What a dreadful time Lady Wallenford has had, my lady. First Virgil's father died, then Virgil almost died at Waterloo, and Virgil's brother passed away soon after that."

Lady Wallenford's head dipped. "Yes, it was dreadful, but now my son is home."

"You've forgotten my sister, Miss Jermyn," Virgil said. "My sister, Dulciana Emma, passed away after my father, Lady Hackwell. Did you know, Mother, Ameline has named her little ones after our Dulciana."

Caroline's low-bodiced gown heaved up and down, as her gaze traveled over the girls to Virgil and back again.

Ameline's cheeks burned. Lady Hackwell sent her a warm smile, and Lord Hackwell leaned back in his chair, his gaze directed at Virgil.

Well, it was plain as day whose children they were.

"A lovely tribute," Lord Hackwell said. "You must have admired the girl, Mrs. Dawes."

She blinked and nodded, unable to speak, and the door opened, bringing in servants with trays of food—biscuits and cakes, plum pudding and sweetmeats—sending the three smaller children squealing.

"Well. It's not just Christmas," Lady Hackwell said. "Today Dee and Em turn three years old. We must celebrate. I so wanted to have a grand dinner with roasted goose, but there now, we'll pretend the fire is a Yule log, and we'll make do with Christmas pudding, and sweets, and lemon syllabub. Will you join us, Lady Wallenford, Miss Jermyn?"

Surely now Lady Wallenford and Caroline would realize they were intruding and leave. And perhaps take Virgil with them.

Lady Wallenford's gaze tracked the girls' movements, color flooding her cheeks and a smile blooming. "We'd be delighted, wouldn't we, Caroline? Caroline's parents don't keep Christmas, but oh, it will be nice to celebrate, and with children to enliven things. And I must have a few moments with my wayward son."

"Indeed," Virgil said dryly, "and I'd be delighted to chat with you."

Virgil leaned close to Ameline. "And we'll chat after that," he whispered. "Do not worry. I won't disappear again."

Her heart clattered. He wouldn't disappear, but could she promise she wouldn't?

Heart sinking, Ameline watched as Lady Wallenford jumped in to help fill plates, wipe spills, and enforce manners as best as possible with the little ones seated on cushions around the table set up by the servants, all the while acting as if Ameline wasn't there.

Lady Wallenford *liked* children. She would want her granddaughters. But not their mother.

Caroline, on the other hand, clutched a delicate bone china plate as though she was deciding whose head to break it on. Except, she would never do something so direct and unladylike.

"Shall we have a song?" Lady Hackwell asked. "A Christmas carol. What say you?"

"A song," Robby and Dee shouted together.

"Ameline, can you manage a tune for us on the pianoforte? Thomas, go and turn back the cover." She beamed a smile at Lady Wallenford. "Mrs. Dawes has been directing our children's choir at Longview, as well as providing instruction in maths, and of course the regular binding up of wounds and salving of scrapes."

"Mrs. Dawes is a woman of many talents," Virgil said.

Her face grew warm enough to make her cheeks itch. "Girls, will you come start off *The First Noel* for Lord and Lady Hackwell?"

As long as no one minded a few mangled verses, the girls could manage. They'd been practicing the song with the other children for the village Christmas celebration before Ameline had been called to London. But singing with a large group of children in a tiny parish church was quite different to performing in a room full of strange lords and ladies. Dee shook her head, and Em pressed her hands against her face.

"I shall sing it," Virgil said, stretching his shoulders back. "Was I not always a good baritone around the campfire, Major?"

Hackwell's laugh filled the room in a way that made Lady Wallenford blanch. Lord Hackwell had been a second son, dragged home from a lifetime in the army by his brother's death, and Lady Hackwell, an eccentric spinster before her marriage. Truly, Virgil's mother must think her son had fallen into a bog spotted with mushrooms.

"I can play." Caroline stood. "I'll play and we can sing together like we used to do, Virgil."

The withering look Virgil sent Caroline buoyed Ameline's spirits.

"Heavens, no, Miss Jermyn," he said. "You are trying to steal a march on the misses who were asked to sing, and I'll not have it. Miss Dulciana and Miss Emma?"

He crossed the room to the girls. Dee raised her jelly-spotted face to his, and he snared a napkin and wiped the corner of her mouth.

Em had frozen at the table, a look on her face so frantic that Ameline smiled her reassurance. Virgil's finger tipped the little chin up and he whispered a few words that made her quiet daughter smile.

Ameline hurried over to the pianoforte. "We shall all sing."

She put some force into her fingers, and the gentlemen gave such a rousing rendition of *The First Noel*, it might have been a battle cry. All of the children, even Thomas joined in at the call to arms.

At the end of the song she looked up to see Caroline frowning at Virgil.

Who was smiling at Ameline.

"Well, how was that?" he asked.

"It would certainly carry to the back pews," Ameline said.

"You are no slouch when it comes to volume, Lord Wallenford," Lady Hackwell said. "And it was great fun, was it not? Steven, you will have to bring your friend along to Longview the next time we visit. He will do the children good."

Ameline's smile vanished. Virgil would not have needed the invitation, but it gave him a good excuse to upset her world. She gave her knuckles an unladylike cracking and flipped hurriedly through the pages while the conversation went on.

"Excellent idea, my love. Wallenford, the cricket field at Longview is top notch, and there are enough children to field proper teams, providing we let the girls play."

"You have girls and boys together at this school? What is this place?" Caroline asked.

"It is the dream of Lady Cathmore and myself," Lady Hackwell said. "And generously supported by Lord Cathmore. It is a home."

"A wonderful home for children," Ameline said. *Her* home, hers and the girls.

"An orphans' home," Lady Wallenford said thoughtfully. "What a noble project."

"And you live at a home for orphans now, Ameline?" There'd been no sarcasm in Lady Wallenford's comment, but Caroline's smug tone sent Ameline's blood roaring.

"Oh no," Lady Hackwell said. "Ameline and her girls have a snug little cottage in the grounds. She comes in and teaches the children, and cleans up their little scratches and scrapes."

"And I serve as a midwife to the parish," Ameline added. "It is a good life, and one I'm grateful for." She straightened the music and placed her fingers on the keys. "Now, *Hark the Herald Angels Sing*. Are you ready?" She might have pounded the piano keys more firmly than needed, but it was better than punching out Caroline's teeth.

She worked her way through the piece, reminding herself that her girls were happy at Longview, and at Mrs. Crawford's, and here. Tonight, they were also petted and fêted by Virgil and his mother, who grasped their hands and sang merrily with them.

Her heart was as jumbled and chaotic as the singing. Dee and Em could have all that attention and love every day.

If Ameline would just give them up.

She blinked through the playing of several songs, hitting the wrong notes occasionally, so fraught with holding her emotion she was relieved to see Jenny slip into the room. After protests and kisses, Jenny led the complaining children away, Thomas, dragging his feet the most. Ameline rose to go with them, but Lady Hackwell stayed her hand and shook her head, inclining her head toward Lady Wallenford, whose gaze trailed the girls again.

"You must not run away," Lady Hackwell whispered.

Ameline's head pounded. She knew. Lady Hackwell knew, had probably even planned this reunion.

Lady Hackwell grinned slyly. "I'd have pointed out the mistletoe hanging over the door when you and Wallenford stepped in, had we had not had our visitors."

Ameline huffed out a breath and shook her head, speechless.

"We will stand with you, Ameline. Do not run," she said.

As soon as the door closed on the children, Virgil's mother turned on him. "I should like a moment of your time, Virgil."

Virgil's shoulders rose in a silent sigh. "Hackwell, might I beg the use of your study?"

"Of course. Come along, I'll take you there." He patted his wife's arm. "Can you spare me a moment, my dear? I'll pop up and make sure Thomas is not giving the nursery maid hell and be back in a bit."

Virgil sent Ameline a nod and a smile and ushered his mother out.

What that nod meant, she couldn't decide. When the door closed, Caroline sat primly and discussed the latest fashions, small talk indeed, given Lady Hackwell's lack of interest in the subject.

For the sake of the Longview girls being trained up as seamstresses, Ameline kept up with Ackermann's and *La Belle Assemblée*, and could match Caroline's observations about sleeves and trims. The knowledge had little impact on her own wardrobe—she dressed simply for her work, but the girls at Longview needed to know what was popular, and just as importantly, what was no longer in style. Lady Hackwell listened politely, turning the conversation to the names of modistes who'd taken in Longview students.

When the topic turned to bonnets, her ladyship sat up straighter, and a ripple passed over her face.

Ameline shot to her feet. Lady Hackwell pressed a hand to her chest, her color rising.

She was in distress. But why?

"Are you well, ma'am?" Caroline asked.

Drat. She'd noticed also.

Caroline sent Ameline an oblique look. "Have you perhaps moved about too soon? I've heard one must stay in bed for a full month after childbirth."

Lady Hackwell clutched a napkin to her chest, opened her mouth, and closed it.

Ameline's breath eased. Lady Hackwell's breasts were full. Double drat these unwelcome visitors. They should have left over an hour ago, instead of lingering to be thorns at a children's celebration.

A distant cry, like the mewling of a cat, reached them.

"Go now, ma'am," Ameline said. "Alton will help you upstairs. I'll entertain Miss Jermyn, and call for the carriage when Lady Wallenford returns."

Lady Hackwell rose. "You are a diamond of the first water, Ameline. Do excuse me, Miss Jermyn."

As the door closed, Caroline turned on Ameline. "Is she ill? Perhaps a real physician is in order."

Yes, perhaps he could come and bleed Lady Hackwell, as Virgil's sister had been bled.

She swallowed her sharp words. "The baby is hungry. She should have been fed a while ago, and Lady Hackwell's milk is coming down. It can be quite uncomfortable, not to mention that it can ruin a gown."

"Oh." Caroline frowned. "Breastfeeding. Whyever? Though I suppose it is fashionable, now."

"Not just fashionable, but forward-thinking. Dr. Smellie recommended it as most conducive to the recovery of the mother and the health of the child, in spite of the discomfort."

Caroline's gaze narrowed. "And you know about this discomfort because you had children. And you named them after Virgil's sister. That was clever of you, Ameline. Or, excuse me, Mrs. Dawes. Where is Mr. Dawes?"

Caroline had dropped her drawing room demeanor and was punching hard.

Ameline's head buzzed with an answering anger. She was sick of the charade she had chosen, sick of pandering to the likes of Caroline Jermyn.

And for the sake of her girls she would keep to the lie. "Mr. Dawes fell at Waterloo."

"How convenient. And you're a widow."

Ameline's fingers curled into fists. "As you would have been, had you married Virgil's brother. Did you drag your feet, Miss Jermyn, when you learned of the marquess's illness? Had you been his widow, you could not later marry your brother-in-law, could you? How convenient."

Caroline bristled. "Those girls are Virgil's."

Her chest tightened. She'd thought they'd been so secretive, so careful, in their love-making, and she'd never revealed her state to anyone at Willowbrook. Oh, but Virgil's brother had speculated and accused.

Caroline's lips quivered on the verge of a smile. "I saw you with him once, in the woods near the folly."

She swallowed around a lump. They'd done no more than kiss that day, and anyway, she had no need to confess to Caroline.

"They are my children, Miss Jermyn, by Mr. Dawes."

"Virgil knows, doesn't he? Yes, I could tell by the way he looked at them." She leaned closer and touched Ameline's arm. "He'll want to bring them up, and his mother is besotted with them already. The bigger one looks just like Virgil's sister, only," she poked a finger at her forehead, "right in the head. Such a relief that must be for Lady Wallenford. She's made it clear she is desperate for grandchildren and she'll want her granddaughters with her. Perhaps they can move with her to the Dower House. One or both can stay on as companions. Until then, they'll be well treated, I promise you that."

Ameline's heart clanged. "*You* promise me that?"

"Yes. Virgil and I are to marry. I shall see that any bastards of his are raised properly. It is not uncommon, after all."

CHAPTER ELEVEN

VIRGIL USHERED HIS MOTHER INTO THE STUDY and seated her near Hackwell's cluttered writing table. Decisive, but not always tidy, was his old commander.

Mother's frown told him all he needed to know of her thoughts. She'd noticed Dulciana's eyes, she'd counted out the months between Ameline's departure and the birth of her daughters.

But life with his father had taught her to talk around what she wanted. If she was true to form, she'd work her way through her small grievances and towards a discussion about Dulciana and Emma.

And she would be frowning more after their talk.

He went to the side table and poured a brandy.

"There's some sherry here, Mother. Would you like some?"

"I need something after this...Virgil, why are you staying here with these...with the Hackwells? Granted, they are charming, but you have a perfectly good townhouse of your own in London and, well, to be honest, they are not good *ton.*"

He bit back a smile. His mother had been away from society for as long as he himself had. That bit of knowledge must have come from the Jermyns.

She accepted her drink and rushed on. "And why did you not *tell* me where you were? I had to threaten to sack Baker to learn your whereabouts."

He turned away grinning. Baker, the long time and long suffering steward of the Lords Wallenford, had given up his employer's location only after obtaining permission. Happy to put the estate back on a proper course after Virgil's brother's death, Baker had forged a true partnership with Virgil, long distance though it was.

"I served under Hackwell at Waterloo," he said. "A capital fellow. Saved my neck more than once. Carried me off the battlefield himself. And his lady has been wonderfully welcoming, in spite of her confinement."

She blinked hard several times and pressed her lips together, hung up on his battlefield injury probably.

Please God, no tears. Waterloo was well behind him. "And as you know, you can't sack Baker. He works for the marquess, not the dowager marchioness."

He tossed back his drink, keeping one eye on her. She dabbed at her eyes with her handkerchief, but the tremble in her lips had transformed into a scowl. *Excellent.*

"Well then, my lord marquess, *you* should let the man go for his parsimonious ways. This gown is three years old. I've had to close up a good part of Willowbrook, and I haven't been up to town since your father died. If not for the kindness of the Jermyns—"

"Speak not to me of the kindness of the Jermyns." Blood roared in his ears. "Especially not the Jermyn sitting in Hackwell's parlour."

She fisted her hands and bit down on her lip. The years of his absence had been hard on her. Her wrinkles had deepened, and gray streaked her hair more abundantly.

And she was still his mother, and Mrs. Crawford had been right. He must at least try to win her over.

Virgil took her glass and his own and set them down. "Mother." He lifted her hand. "You have dishes groaning with food, and servants to fetch them. The tenants' cottages have all been repaired, and all of them eat every day. The previous Lords Wallenford did not manage well, and the post-war years have been hard, for many people, not just you. *I* forced the economies. Baker merely carried them out. When Parliament resumes this spring, you may come up for a quiet season, and when you return to Willowbrook, you shall have all that you need at the Dower House."

Her head shot up. "But you will need a hostess…" She caught her breath, a smile blooming on her face, and she looked quite like the woman who used to sometimes tuck him in at night.

"You're thinking of taking a wife. I'm so happy." She squeezed his hand. "Now, Caroline—"

"Not Caroline."

His abrupt tone caught her up. "Why ever not. It's been understood she would marry—"

"The marquess. So she told me. And yet she dragged her feet with the previous marquess. She could have married him months before his death, yet she didn't. Doesn't that seem strange to you, Mother?"

She paled. "He was ill with an ague."

It had been no ague. His brother's fondness for brothels had finally caught up with him, but if she truly didn't know, he would leave her that fiction. "And he wished to delay the wedding?"

She wrung her hands together. "She persuaded him it was better to wait until he recovered. Virgil, you cannot disregard a bride such as Caroline, an only child and the estate not entailed. And she cares for you. She admitted to me that you were her first love."

"Did she indeed?" He sighed. "I'm not at all convinced that Caroline cares for anything but a title, Mother. Let her go and find another one."

Her brow wrinkled and she moved closer. "She's given up so much for our family. So much time. She is not as young as she once was. Though it was you she cared for, when duty called, she gave you up. And then your brother died, and you went off and were wounded. It's a very sensible match, and the right thing to do. It's a matter of *justice*."

He raised an eyebrow. "Justice, Mother? Justice for Caroline Jermyn?"

She swallowed and her gaze flitted to a spot over his shoulder, and he could see the wheels turning inside her head.

It was the shoulder that had borne the brunt of a bullet, and it damn well ached under this onslaught of emotion.

"Why did you stay away so long, Virgil?"

Pain laced through her voice, as if she'd suffered too.

Dammit, she'd been part of the problem. "I was on the king's business, Mother."

"Because you *wanted* to stay away."

He let out a tight breath. "Yes. That too."

She shook her head. "You *will* marry Caroline."

"Will I?"

"You must have an heir, and Caroline will do. She knows everyone in the district, and she and her family are known in the *ton*. She will help you politically. When she was born, her mother and I talked. Caroline was raised to be Lady Wallenford, if it could be possible. Oh truly, with your brother dying, and you staying away so long leaving her hoping, the Wallenfords have not been fair to her."

"I see."

She clutched his arm. "I'm so glad. We can call the banns—"

He held up a hand. "Not so fast. What of our fairness to Ameline Illington?"

Her smile crumpled and she searched his face. "Those children...You were with her and them today—" She put a hand to her chest. "Those children are yours, aren't they? What have you done?"

He took her hand gently. "Nothing yet. But tell me, Mother, what did you, and my brother, and your Caroline do to Miss Illington three-and-a-half years ago after I left?"

She blinked twice and took in a breath.

"Why did you send her away, Mother?"

"I didn't. Your brother said she had to go. He said she'd seduced you, that she was angling to marry you. I didn't believe it, but now I see those girls—"

"You let him cast her off, pregnant with your grandchildren—twins, mother, and you know how hard that is—without a reference or wages."

"I *didn't* know...I...I gave her what money I could." She shook her head and smiled wryly. "I did always like her. She was so good for Dulciana. Had I known, I would have acted, I swear it." Her brow furrowed and she glanced away. "They are beautiful girls. Your daughters." She shook her head again. "So many lost years."

"Yes. Very good, Mother. You've recognized my daughters, and all the lost time. That part of this matter is long ago done and I can't recapture those years. And I should like your help with what comes next, though in truth you have no say in it. I intend to take care of Ameline and my daughters."

"Take care of—" She pressed her lips together and began to pace. "Of course, the girls can live quietly with us—er, with me for a while, until they're old enough for school and you've had your own children. And then perhaps Caroline will allow them to visit for holidays. But to keep Ameline as a...a mistress, at least at the start of your marriage—"

"We are done here, Mother." This was, perhaps, impossible. Charm wouldn't do the trick. Perhaps it would take a miracle. In any case, before he could move his mother's thoughts on to Ameline, he'd have to dispose of Caroline. "Come along."

He took her elbow and ushered her to the door. It was like pulling a stone statue on wheels, but they soon enough reached the drawing room door, and Virgil opened it to the sound of Caroline's voice.

"...can move with her to the Dower House. One or both can stay as companions. Until then, they'll be well treated, I promise you that."

Caroline's smug tone sent his blood roaring. He dropped his mother's arm and pushed the door wider.

"*You* promise me that?" Ameline's laugh was a tight, choked sound.

"Yes."

Caroline sat with her back to the door, but Ameline had spotted him and locked eyes with him.

"Virgil and I are to marry. I shall see that any bastards of his are raised properly. It is not uncommon, after all."

CHAPTER TWELVE

AMELINE'S SMILE WAS NOT AT ALL WARM, BUT it heartened him. She'd not dissolved into tears, or reached over to scratch out Caroline's eyes. She would be a good partner—the best of partners. If only he could convince her to not run away again.

"Virgil." Caroline jumped to her feet, color rising in her cheeks. "I did not expect you back so soon. I suppose you heard our conversation and you must know, I would not hold any children born out of wedlock against you. I will see to the care of the girls and any others you may have. I understand about gentlemen, I do, though I would hope…"

Her chattering petered off and she frowned between him and his mother.

"Others? You think there are others besides Dulciana and Emma?" He laughed. "You must have me mixed up with your late fiancé."

Ameline got to her feet. "I wish you luck, Virgil. And my daughters will not—"

"*Don't* leave, Ameline. Please. Don't. I'm not going to marry you, Miss Jermyn, and if you think to coerce me by moving my mother into your home to stir gossip of an impending engagement, you will be greatly disappointed."

Silence met him, though he could see Caroline's face softening as she conjured up a way to wheedle him. He was having none of it.

"Shall we talk about what *you* did to Ameline, Miss Jermyn?"

"What she *did*?" his mother asked.

"Nor should you feign innocence, Mother. When Baker could find no trace of Ameline, I wrote to you, in case you might know something, and in the very next letter from your eldest, he enclosed a note to me from Ameline. Only it wasn't written by Ameline, was it?" He shook his head. "You should have thought about how distinctive your penmanship is, Miss Jermyn, when you wrote me that letter last month, begging me to return home to mother."

"I declare, I don't know what you're talking about." Caroline sounded breathless, her sharp look belying the the innocent tone of her words. "I wrote you a letter asking you to return because your mother was in despair."

Gasping, his mother drew herself up. "*You* wrote to Virgil about *me*?"

She hadn't known about Caroline's ploy to bring him home. Well, and perhaps she hadn't known about the first letter either.

"I...I..." Caroline fumbled for words. "My mother and I thought...."

"Really, Caroline?" His mother's lips trembled, and her face paled. "What was the first letter, Virgil?"

He spotted Ameline inching toward the door and reeled her back gently. "I'm not going to marry Caroline," he told her. "She'll not go anywhere near our children. And be assured, Dulciana and Emma are my only children."

"Caroline, what letter did you write in Ameline's name?" Tension laced through his mother's voice.

Caroline's color rose even higher. "I...I...my lady, we've stayed well past our welcome. My mother will be expecting us home already."

Caroline wanted to leave? Excellent. Still holding on to Ameline, Virgil opened the door and all but bumped in to Alton.

"Pardon, my lord," the butler said. "Mrs. Dawes, Mrs. Crawford has sent a young man and a carriage for you."

Heat flared in him. "A young man?"

Instantly diverted, Ameline tugged at his arm. "Her grandson. Tell him I'll come at once, Alton." She turned back to Virgil, her dark eyes searching his. "I must go."

He thought of the swollen young woman in the bed under the eaves. "Is it about Miss Smith?"

"Yes. It must be." She swallowed and glanced at his mother and back to him. "But, the girls—"

"Will be here. I promise."

Chewing her lip, she fixed her gaze on his shoulder, and he could see her deciding whether to trust him.

"They will be here. I promise," he whispered.

She took a deep breath and nodded.

A sprig of greenery fell upon his arm and he glanced up.

Ameline's gaze followed his and he heard her gasp.

"Mistletoe," he said. "How providential."

She frowned, and her mouth opened. He pressed his lips to hers, cutting off a protest.

Ameline's arms flailed, but he cupped her head and held the kiss a moment longer.

"Virgil," his mother cried.

He straightened and looked into wide dark eyes. "They will be here."

She licked her lips, nodded, and slipped out.

He signaled Alton to call the Jermyns' carriage.

His mother stood wringing her hands and frowning. "Who is Miss Smith?" she asked. "And what is this about a letter? What is going on?"

He ushered both ladies to the hall, where a servant had gathered their pelisses.

"Miss Smith is a patient with a difficult pregnancy."

"And they've called Ameline instead of a physician?" Caroline asked.

He rubbed his hands together. Devil take it, if he'd been a man like his father, he would have slapped Caroline, here, in Hackwell's hall, in front of the servants. Instead, he reached for his mother's pelisse, holding it out for her. "An accoucheur is attending also."

Mother crossed her arms over her chest like a child. "No. No, no, no. I am not finished here."

A servant opened the front door announcing the arrival of the Jermyns' carriage.

Hackwell picked that moment to rejoin them. "Heading off, I see. Nice of you to visit, my lady, Miss Jermyn. Hope you've settled all of your business."

"We have *not*," his mother said. She yanked the pelisse out of Virgil's hands, and handed it back to the servant. "I must beg your hospitality a bit longer, Lord Hackwell."

"But the carriage is here, my lady," Caroline said. "And Mother will be—"

"Go then," Mother said, for the first time in many years, sounding sure of herself. He hadn't realized how much she'd wallowed in meekness, *weakness* from the years of being beaten down by his father and brother. "But I'm staying. I will know what this letter is which you deny writing, that has my son so angry. I will not leave."

He wouldn't be one more Wallenford bully, not with her.

He took her hand. Perhaps he could convince her to move lodgings entirely and get her out of the grip of the helpful Jermyns. She could have his own very well-appointed room. The Hackwells must have another free bed somewhere...Yes, of course, there was a large one right down the corridor from his own with room for one more.

"Of course you may stay, Lady Wallenford." Hackwell had Caroline's arm, escorting her to the door. "Do not worry, Miss Jermyn, Lady Wallenford may have free use of my carriage." He turned and flashed Virgil a grin that had him wiping his own face, fighting a smile.

"Come along then, Mother, and we'll try this talking business again."

The glowing fog of the short December morning shed a weak light through the dormer windows as Ameline wiped scurf and fluids from the small raging body in front of her. The kicks, the startled, tight breaths, the vacant screams, made her blink back tears. The little one's panic was too much like his mother's, too fresh, too stark. Between Baxter and Mrs. Crawford, they'd managed to bring out the child and the afterbirth. God only knew how.

She forced her fingers to the familiar work, cleaning, comforting, counting fingers and toes, and the moments until the wet nurse arrived.

And then she'd move on to a familiar task, made unfamiliar—cleaning the new mother.

The newly deceased mother. Despite all their efforts, Miss Smith's breathing had just stopped.

Ameline held the baby close and wiped tears with the back of her hand. She'd spent the last frantic moments praying as she hadn't prayed since she'd watched Virgil's sister fade after her last bleeding.

Baxter's two fingers came away from the young woman's neck, and Mrs. Crawford put down the wrist she was pressing. They moved aside and conferred in low, somber tones, while the maid, Aggie, stood pressed to the wall, tears streaming.

Death in childbirth was common enough, but Ameline had never yet lost one of her new mothers. She'd never dealt with this part.

At least the poor babe had survived, yet this little boy would grow up never knowing the woman who'd given him life.

Impulsively, she settled the child onto his mother's chest and his crying paused.

Miss Smith's eyes fluttered and she drew in a sharp breath.

"She's alive," Aggie shouted.

Virgil rubbed his sore backside and rose from the padded settee. The tea Mrs. Crawford's granddaughter brought him had gone cold hours ago, but he didn't have the heart, or truth be told, the appetite to bother anyone for a fresh pot. The narrow townhouse had been creaking and twittering all night with footsteps going up and down stairs, muffled shouts from above, and whispered conversations passing outside the parlour.

He'd arrived before midnight, his business with his mother settled, his business with Ameline ready to commence as soon as *her* business with Miss Smith was completed. The dense fog had lifted—it must be close to noon now.

Another cry floated down the hall staircase.

He swiped a hand through his hair. Hell. Two of these ordeals within one week—how did Ameline do this?

He balled his fist. Perhaps it was good he hadn't been here when the twins were born. It might have killed him knowing she was suffering so, knowing the risk to her life. And wasn't he just another selfish cad?

Damn, but he wished he'd brought a flask.

He limped to the window and back. Well, he was here for her now, here for Miss Smith too, suffering along with both of them, whether they wanted his support or not.

Hell, he'd even bent a knee when no one was looking. Only the one, since his bad leg, the one sliced by the French saber, would have protested, but he hoped that would be enough.

The whispers told him all was not well. All the Christmas jolliness of Mrs. Crawford's home had evaporated, the pine boughs and ribbons drooping, the fire sputtering, and a pall like the dense fog of the earlier December morning had settled.

A cat wailed somewhere outside, and Virgil grabbed a poker and stabbed at the coals. If it didn't stop soon, he'd go find the damn feline himself and end the caterwauling.

Upstairs, a door creaked, and the crying grew louder.

His heart lifted. Not a cat—a baby, a crying, breathing, living baby.

Feet raced down the stairs, all the way down to the kitchen, he would guess and then more resounded on their way up.

Mrs. Crawford's granddaughter flew in, panting. "She's alive. She was dead, but she's alive."

Panic seized him. *Ameline.*

But no…that was mad. "The baby?"

The girl shook her head, catching her breath. "It's a boy."

He blinked, trying to keep up. "Miss Smith was dead?"

The girl beamed a smile at him. "Gran says it's a miracle."

Virgil sank back onto the hard settee and cradled his face in his hands. Another miracle this day. Now he just needed one more.

An older maid came and slapped a fresh pot of tea and some biscuits down, and hurried out. Back to the kitchen probably, to boil more pots of water for Ameline.

He smiled, and then laughed, remembering his encounter with her on the servants' stairs a few nights earlier. *Give me the blasted bucket, Virgil.* Such a romantic use of his name after so many years apart. And where the hell was she now?

He paced, and paced, and paced, hearing the change in the house as the tension lifted. She would be tired after her long night. He mustn't pressure her. He mustn't ask her until she'd had some rest. But then he wouldn't wait one moment longer.

"Go on then." Mrs. Crawford patted Ameline's arm. "Have a cup in the parlour and one of the boys'll send for a hackney."

She washed her hands one more time and looked at Miss Smith, who was taking dribbles of broth while she watched her baby suckling at the wet nurse's breast. With fresh bedding and linens, and the tension drained out of her face, the young mother looked like she might pull through. Baxter had departed not long ago. Perhaps Ameline *could* leave now also.

Or—perhaps she should stay. Mrs. Crawford and Aggie had been up all night as well.

"She's not out of danger," Ameline whispered. So much could go wrong—puerperal fever, a hemorrhage, or God forbid, a seizure.

"There are plenty of us to sit with her. Go home to your girls."

She sighed. "All right." Hackwell House was not home, but her girls were there, so that was where she would go. "I'll check on them and have a rest. And I can come back if you need me."

Mrs. Crawford shooed her out the door and she descended the narrow stairs.

The hall was empty, but she could feel the warmth coming from the open parlour door. She'd just have that spot of tea and then find her own way back to Mayfair.

As she stepped into the parlour, Virgil shot from his seat.

She rubbed her eyes. "You're here," she said. "Why are you here?" Alarm spiked through her. "The girls—"

"Are fine. I'm here because I promised."

"Promised?"

"Promised Miss Smith she and her babe would be cared for."

Her heart sank. He'd come for Miss Smith.

He crossed the room and took both of her hands. "And I came for you. Was it very awful?"

She bit her lip and thought of the young woman's struggle to birth the baby and then the placenta, and then the great rush of blood...from a uterine atony, Baxter called it. Floppy uterus, Mrs. Crawford said, going to work on Miss Smith's belly. And all along, the worry of a seizure.

In truth, her heart quaked at the thought of facing such a delivery again. Though she would. Of course she would.

Strong arms pulled her and her cheek touched smooth warm wool that smelled of bay rum, and coal smoke, and Virgil. A sob wracked her and she tried to pull away, but his big hand flattened on the middle of her back, and she was just like that baby bawling upstairs.

"There, there." Virgil patted her back. "It *must* have been completely dreadful to make my Ameline cry."

She stiffened and her heart began to pound. *His* Ameline.

Yes, she was his. From the first moment he'd walked into his sister Dulciana's rooms, she'd been his. Her heart would always be his, but she couldn't let him know that.

And it was a horrifying delivery, and he would use that fact to hound her about abandoning midwifery, so she could rest like a coward on his shoulder every moment he could spare from his life as a great lord, every moment he could spare from the proper wife he would find to bear him a proper heir, because he could never marry a woman who worked as a midwife.

She stepped back and wiped her eyes. "I should like to go back to Hackwell House now." The girls would be there, her touchstones, her babies, her life.

CHAPTER THIRTEEN

ON THEIR RIDE BACK TO HACKWELL HOUSE, Virgil sat across from Ameline. Her eyes were closed, but he knew she wasn't sleeping, not with that ramrod posture.

He'd rushed things. He'd not been able to help taking her into his arms, and then he'd gone and questioned her about her difficult night, and...damn, this was going to be harder than he'd suspected.

Best to have it out then. He came from a household of conflict dodgers. The Marquess of Wallenford declared what must be and everyone was expected to shut up and fall in line. His mother had certainly gone with that approach, and her silent, resentful acquiescence had been the one reliable current flowing through Willowbrook.

But this Marquess of Wallenford wasn't going to have that sort of marriage. Dammit, he'd rather have a bloody good blow now and again, than live with a woman suffering in heartsick silence.

As soon as she'd had a good night's sleep.

The carriage slowed to a stop and he handed her out. "I'll take you right to the nursery."

She lifted a tired gaze. "I know the way."

"So you do. But I want to see them also."

Ameline dragged herself ahead of him up the stairs and as they neared the attic landing, she could hear the clamor of voices and loud laughter.

A sense of relief and rightness came over her. The noise reminded her of the children at Longview, playing happily during their free time. Her girls had settled in and were having fun, and she had nothing to worry about. Virgil and his mother hadn't whisked them away or turned their little lives sour. Not yet, anyway.

She went through the nursery door and her heart plummeted. Lady Wallenford sat at the nursery table, head thrown back in a laugh, a child perched on her knee.

Her child.

Across the table, Dee lifted her mossy gaze and shouted "Mama." Em craned her body over Lady Wallenford's arm and smiled a greeting.

"Look, Mama," Dee said. "My name."

She became aware of Virgil's hand steadying her and shook it off, approaching the table.

Lady Hackwell's boys were there also. Thomas lolled in a chair, a book spread open on the table before him. Across from him, Robby gripped a pencil.

"Look." Dee poked the paper, where someone had printed out the letters of her first name. Below them was a scrawl of squiggles. "Dee, dee, dee," she said. "My name."

"Me, too." Em stubbed her finger on the paper where E-M-M-A had been neatly printed, crosshatched lines below simulating the letters above.

"They know some of their letters," Lady Wallenford said, beaming. "You are doing marvelously, girls."

Dee's lower lip jutted out. "Mine's too long."

"Do not fret, Dulciana," Lady Wallenford said. "The task will be equal when we start writing your last name, Radcliffe."

Ameline opened her mouth to object, but her throat had constricted, and the room spun. Virgil's arm came round her waist, and against her will, she leaned into him.

Lady Wallenford's face softened. "I'm so sorry. The birth...was it..."

"Miss Smith is fine," Virgil said, "as is her newborn son."

"Thank heavens. And you both look done in. Did you get any rest at all? No, I suppose not. Ameline, you must sleep for a while. Lord Hackwell has gone out, and Lady Hackwell has promised an informal dinner tonight which Master Thomas will be allowed to attend *if* he finishes today's lessons." She sent Thomas a smile that signaled she might be subject to wheedling. "I'm seeing to his lessons and keeping an eye on Robby and my grand...on the girls."

Ameline blinked. She'd been about to say her granddaughters.

But...Lady Wallenford was supervising the nursery, not just because of the girls. From the very moment she'd held Lady Hackwell's newborn, she'd shown a genuine interest in all the children.

And planned to stay through the rest of this afternoon and into the evening.

An ache started behind Ameline's eyes and began to pulse.

She looked around the room. Jenny sat in a chair supposedly working on mending, but in reality watching the goings-on with great interest. The maid sent her a broad smile.

Mary must be with the baby, and perhaps Lady Hackwell was down in the parlour entertaining. "Is...is Miss Jermyn visiting also?"

Lady Wallenford took in a deep breath and sent her son a long look.

"No, my dear," she said. "She's not here. Virgil will explain everything. Now, give your mama a kiss, girls. She must go and have a nap."

A round of boisterous hugging and kissing followed. At the door of the nursery, Lady Wallenford gripped both of Ameline's hands and looked at her misty-eyed. She opened her mouth, shut it, and opened it again. "Virgil will explain everything."

Had Ameline's brain not been so mired in fatigue, she would have seen Lady Wallenford's next move.

A hug. Virgil's mother smelled like lilies and clean linen. Once, only once, Ameline had seen her hug her daughter Dulciana like this.

She beat back a sudden rush of moisture to her eyes.

"No one will take your girls from you," Lady Wallenford whispered.

Ameline drew in a deep breath, disentangled herself and stepped back, knocking into Virgil, who captured her elbows and steadied her yet again.

In front of her, Lady Wallenford's gaze held compassion. Behind her, warmth pulsed from the lady's son, overwhelming her, sending shivers through her.

There must be a fire in the grate, because the children looked warm. Was she the only one here feeling chilled?

Caught between a marquess and a marchioness, she was glad to see Jenny put aside her mending and stand. "You do look tired, Mrs. Dawes. I can go with you and—"

"No," Virgil said. "You'll stay here with my mother, else we'll find Thomas daring one of these nestlings to go out of the window and peck about on the roof."

Jenny curled her lips in squashing a smile, while Thomas eyed the window.

Ameline hugged herself, fighting to stay calm and upright. "Thank you, Jenny. I can manage."

She kissed the girls one more time and left.

Virgil trailed her down the stairs, close enough she could feel his heat.

Heart quaking, she gripped the banister more tightly. He intended to bring all those hot male humors into her bedchamber, and probably lend her more than his shoulder.

The blood pounding through her lightened her step and made her giddy. She wanted him to follow. She wanted *him*. And that was so wrong. She needed to forget what they'd had, forge her own path, make her own life. She'd proven she could, and she needed to carry on.

Virgil will talk to you. What the devil was Lady Wallenford going on about? Care of the girls probably, and how would that work, if no one would take them from her?

Her foot wobbled, but she righted herself just as his hand steadied her, sending more heat through her.

Blast it. She was like the beggar standing under the baker's window smelling the bread baking and with no honest way to a loaf of her own. She'd years ago squelched all that hunger, sealed it up right and tight, with bitter memories and hard cold facts.

But this night's drama—a child surviving a hard labor, a mother's miraculous rise from the dead, Lady Wallenford's unaccountable promise, all that was chipping away at the hard husk that was Ameline's heart.

And there'd also been Virgil's wide shoulder.

She paused at the landing and gave her head a small shake. After such a night, and with so little sleep, who wouldn't feel hopeful?

And she was being ridiculous. She was the foolish woman who'd borne a reckless lord's bastards. That would not taint her for life. She would not let it, nor would she succumb to some tender dream that would put her back where she'd started. No more foolish romance.

She lifted her chin and mustered the energy to speak firmly. "You've just put an awful idea into Thomas's head."

Virgil smiled, totally oblivious to her mood. "Oh, I guarantee you, he's had the idea already."

"How would you know?"

"Well, I'm a boy too."

His grin was indeed so boyish it made her laugh.

He was reckless and she was a fool.

She stopped at the door of her bedchamber and turned to him, intending to say goodnight with some dignity.

Her foot turned in her half-boot again, and she swayed toward the door.

He caught her up in his arms. "You're dead on your feet. You were up all night, weren't you?"

"So were you."

"No. I spent the night on Mrs. Crawford's quite firm settee. Put my backside right to sleep, it did, and the rest of me managed to doze a bit also. Come then."

He whisked her through the door, ran a hand down her back, and laughed.

"Aren't you the clever one," he said, turning her around. "You've got all the hooks and pins and whatnots in the front."

Her hands flew to her chest. "Virgil—"

"I'm not going to ravish you in this state." He gazed at her gravely, and she dropped her hands.

"Good." He went to work undressing her. "Mother told you I'd explain."

The dress slipped to the floor and cold air touched her arms and back, making her shiver.

Virgil's arms wrapped around her and he eased her closer to the grate. Once there, near the low fire, he released her and ran his hot hands over her bare arms. "Now, I'll just get these infernal stays off you and put on more coal."

His fingers working so close to her middle sent butterflies through her at each touch. The stays loosened but her breathing still came in tight shivering gasps. He slipped the corset down and she stepped out of it, clad only in her chemise, stockings, and half-boots.

Virgil looked her up and down, heating her without touching. She could fling herself at him and be in his arms, and feel safe, whole, loved.

A tremble rolled through her, one that came from a place deep inside, and she wrapped herself in a tight hug. Best not to go down the path of loving Virgil, not again, not if she wanted to keep her post and profession.

He moved behind her, pulled off her cap and began scattering the pins that held up her plait and the ribbon tie at the end, finally raking his fingers through her hair until it cascaded around her.

His breath was hot on the back of her head, his pulse pounding against her shoulder.

"Come," he whispered, touching her arms, sending new shivers through her. "Let's get you to bed."

To bed with Virgil.

She dug in her heels. "What were you supposed to tell me?"

She could feel him tensing, sense the struggle in him. That night in her room, if the girls hadn't woken, he would have taken her then, and he could do so now. She could feel all of *that* conversation going on between them.

His hands loosened, and his breathing eased. "Mother and I had a long talk last night. She recognized the girls as mine, right away. And she's moved lodgings to Hackwell House."

"What?" Her mind raced. There was something missing in between the last two sentences.

"It seemed best all around. Now," he led her to the bed and pulled back the covers. "Get in."

When she lifted her feet onto the bed he caught sight of her stockings and shoes.

In quick surgical motions, he had her half-boots off, her garters loose and her stockings peeled off. But the way he was biting his lip, it was costing him.

And her. The touch of his hand on her leg had sent her insides pooling.

That wouldn't do. "The Hackwells know also," she said, swinging her legs onto the bed.

"Yes. For how long I don't know." Virgil tucked her in and let out an agonized breath, as if he had just survived a tooth-pulling.

And she felt his pain gratefully. There'd be no amorous congress for them tonight, and it was just as well. They had no future together. "I believe the Hackwells already guessed it before either of us arrived here."

He smoothed her hair back and his serious look made her want to cry. He was everything she wanted in a man, and she couldn't have him, and they both knew it. She would have to face the future, not as his lover but as a woman who shared parenthood with him.

"Do the girls know?" she asked.

"No." He picked up her hand and chafed it. "I should like to be there when you tell them. I want to see how they react, hear what they say. I want to answer their questions if they have any." He dropped a kiss on her forehead and she struggled to breathe. He'd left it to her to tell them, and that was something.

She watched the play of his muscles as he bent over the hearth and desire rippled through her, sending her burrowing deeper into the bedding.

She must not look at Virgil. She must not think about him, or invite him to her bed. He had his own room...or...Lady Wallenford had moved here. Wherever was she staying? She supposed in this grand house there were a few more bedchambers, maybe not as fine as this one and the one Virgil occupied.

The pain in her head dulled to an ache and her eyes slipped closed. Lady Wallenford wanted to know her granddaughters. They would be loved, and coddled, and pampered by a marchioness, and was that so bad?

As long as Lady Wallenford kept her promise, and Ameline didn't lose them entirely.

A rumbling noise permeated Ameline's sleep, a soft weight on her middle. The girls had crawled into bed with her again, one lying on top, and one snuggled next to her.

She didn't mind, not truly, especially on cold nights when it was hard to heat the cottage's small bed chamber. But this night wasn't so cold. One needn't pull the covers over her head to stay warm, and on such a night it was better they slept in their own bed together. She must get up and move them, but just for a moment she wanted to feel the closeness.

She patted the weight and expected the soft touch of a child's plump bottom.

Ameline's eyes flew open. This was a hand, connected to an arm and—

She turned her head. "Virgil. What are you doing here?"

His eyes stayed closed but he smiled lazily. "I *was* sleeping."

She raised up on her elbows. The fire was mere embers, and sun streamed in through the windows.

"What time is it?"

His hand wrapped her waist, snugging her closer through a leisurely yawn. When she looked, he gazed back at her, a dark boggy look that sent her blood pounding.

"By God, you're beautiful in the morning, love."

Her breath caught. He was the beautiful one, even with wild hair and stubble. Perhaps especially with that. She fisted the sheet and kept her hand still.

Was it morning? Was anyone about? Had a maid seen them together?

He shifted, and every nerve on the side of her body sprang to life, trying to reach him.

But someone might come in.

Her mind raced, snatching at memories. They'd returned in the afternoon, the gloomy light had been slipping away and...the nursery. Lady Wallenford had been there. Virgil had undressed her.

Panic flooded her. What had she done?

Her chemise had crawled up and bunched at her waist, as it usually did.

She reached a hand under the covers and began to adjust her hem.

Virgil chuckled. He still wore his shirt, granted that it flopped open and was more off than on, revealing his uninjured shoulder, and a stretch of muscled chest scattered with dark hair. The sheet covered the rest of him, and she itched to pull it back to see if he still wore his trousers.

Warmth uncurled in her. Desire. Blatant, wanton, raging need.

She bit her lip and closed her eyes.

"Lay back down, love. I'll put more coal on the fire."

"Wait." She stayed his hand and rolled toward him. A lock of hair fell over one slitted eye while he gazed back.

No fire was needed. There was plenty of heat here. She touched a finger to his jaw and scraped it over the stubble there.

"Or I'll just stay here and keep you warm," he said, his voice huskier than usual.

It was now or never.

"I'm destined to be ruined again." She pressed her lips to his.

The sweet touch of her lips sent the flames burning inside higher.

They'd slept the night through, or rather she had, her breasts rising up and down, easy breaths passing in and out through the lips plundering his now.

Inside his britches, his cock leaped in delight. It had woken him several times during the night, long before the avian one Hackwell must keep in the mews.

She rolled against him and froze.

Her head lifted away from his lips, hair dangling everywhere in a messy abandon that brought the girl he'd tupped in a carriage back to him, eyes glowing impossibly dark, just like then.

When her leg shifted against his swollen member, one corner of her mouth twisted up.

"Good God," he said.

She cupped his jaw in her warm palm. "Just…just this once. But will you withdraw?"

"Withdraw?" Desire soared in him, and his hips flexed against her. A man could only take so much.

"Yes." She bent to kiss him, but he pulled back, and those swollen lips compressed in a frown. She let out a breath and rolled onto her back. "We can only do this once. And we shouldn't. But when we do, I don't wish to be with child. It took only a few times the last time, if you'll remember."

He swallowed a smile. Well, that made sense. Perhaps it was even sensible for a while.

But he had something he must say before they proceeded and—

The door latch clicked and giggling poured in, along with two little girls.

Ameline shrieked and scuttled away.

"Mama." Dee catapulted onto the bed, her skirts tangling around her.

"Oh, dear."

That voice was Lady Wallenford's.

Ameline flung off Virgil's hand, pulling the covers higher, while Virgil, his shirt crawling down both arms and baring all of his chest, sat up and grabbed Emma.

"You rascals have woken your mama," he said.

They erupted in giggles, as if finding him in their mama's bed was no surprise. Well, and he'd been there a few nights ago hadn't he?

"Lady Wallenford," Ameline said, "I...I..."

When she dared to look, she saw that his mother had gone pale. And of course she had, finding her son in the arms of a lover.

"Mother," Virgil said. "None of this is Ameline's fault, and I haven't had a chance to—"

"Virgil," her voice cracked. "My boy." She covered her mouth and stared at him, blinking back tears.

"Oh," Ameline tugged his shirt back over the scar.

"Oh, that." He waved a hand. "Now you've seen it, don't fret. It's all healed."

"Is it?" His mother's voice shook.

"We go to the park," Dee interrupted. "With her," she said, pointing at his mother.

Ameline pulled Dee over. "We do not point," she said gently. "And that is Lady Wallenford." She bit her lip and took a deep breath. "She is your grandmama. Your real granny."

Dee's eyes grew wide and for once she was silenced.

"Who's he?" Emma pointed at Virgil.

Leave it to her quiet one to ask the most important question.

Virgil took Em's finger and nipped it, sending her into more giggles.

"This is your papa," Ameline said.

His mother whooshed out a breath and clapped her hands together, eyes shining. "Then it is settled. Ameline, I should like to talk to you later. Or," she slid her gaze over to Virgil, "tomorrow when Virgil goes out. I shall help you however I can. I know there will be much to learn and I can —"

"Mother."

Lady Wallenford's eyes widened. "You haven't... Oh, you did say you hadn't—"

"We just woke."

She blinked. "You slept almost the clock round. Well, of course you did. Mrs. Crawford sent a note to say that Miss Smith was stronger this morning. I...I hope you can forgive me, Ameline. I hope we can be friends."

Robby ran in with Jenny on his heels. The maid caught the boy and snatched him by the collar. "Beg pardon, Mrs. Dawes. An' you run like this at the park, Master Robby, an' you won't be going again soon, nor seein' the monkey dance today."

"Mukkey," Dee shouted.

"The monkey." Ameline pushed the covers, and then remembered her undress and pulled them back up. "He's here in the square? I can be ready in but a moment and come with you."

"No," Lady Wallenford said. "I mean, yes, an organ grinder is in the square. Dulciana mentioned you saw him the day you arrived. But don't worry, one of the footmen will accompany Jenny and me. Come now, girls, kiss your mama and papa."

As soon as they'd left, Ameline was hauled without ceremony back into his arms.

"I—we should go with them, Virgil. Such excitement—"

"No." He tucked a stray lock of hair behind her ear. "Let Mother take them, and they'll have double the fun telling us about it." He nuzzled her ear, sending a warm buzz through her. "Here's the thing, Ameline. I've never stopped loving you. Will you marry me?"

Her skin rippled at his touch but rising desire battled a different emotion, one she couldn't quite name—fear? Or shame? Or anger?

His mother and their girls had just discovered them in bed together. Virgil was boxing her in, or so he thought.

And if she made love to him...

She took a deep breath. "That was a rather abrupt proposal."

"Yes, well, no telling who might run in and interrupt. What say you? Will you make me the happiest of men?"

"The happiest of men," she said, flatly.

"Yes, and I will do everything in my power to make you the happiest of women."

She dropped her gaze and fought for breath. Oh, to be held by him, kissed by him every night. To watch him raising his girls and loving them also...

But life wasn't lived in a vacuum. Now he was back, he would take up his seat in the Lords. He would need connections, the kind of connections a high-born wife could provide.

"No, Virgil. I can't."

His grip loosened and his finger traced a lazy trail down her neck. "Is it because you don't love me?"

He held her gaze a long moment, lifting all of his masks, and what she saw there made her heart flip.

Virgil truly did love her, and more fool he.

There'd been enough deception and lies. She curled up and rested her forehead on her knees. She couldn't look at him and say what she must. "I love you." Pain sliced through her. "And I love my daughters. And I love my work." She choked. "And I love you. But I don't want to be a marchioness. I don't want to run a big house, and run the gauntlet of cuts at society events, and run to the modiste every week."

"That is a great deal of running. I could see it would tire you."

She choked in a breath, and he pulled her down into his arms.

His fingers found a knot under one of her shoulder blades and kneaded it, while she rattled against him trying hard not to cry.

She wanted this. She wanted him. But she didn't want to give up the young ladies like Miss Smith.

"I see that this is too much, too soon. Mother wants me to visit Doctors' Commons tomorrow, but I can see you must have time to think about it."

"I've thought about it," she mumbled against his shoulder, "and the answer is no."

"You know," he found another knot and went to work, making her groan, "I don't give a fig about routs and balls, and as for politics, I'll enter the Lords with men I respect, Hackwell, and Cathmore, and there are others. Hackwell has some scheme about helping poor children and their mothers, and he'll bloody well need someone to stand shoulder to shoulder with him."

She'd heard Lady Hackwell speak of it. "And will you, Virgil? Will you stand with him?"

"Indeed I will. But it will be easier if I have a wife with something in her head besides frippery. Plus, Baker says Willowbrook still doesn't have a midwife, and it is high time that changes."

He went silent and his hand stilled. She could feel his heart beating in tune with her own while she tried to make sense of his words.

Willowbrook needed a midwife. She wouldn't have to be the marchioness. She could move back to Willowbrook, and the girls could visit him.

Her heart sank. Him and his wife. "I cannot do it, Virgil. I cannot come be the village midwife for you." She tried to pull away but he held her.

"No, but as the marchioness you can help whoever you select to be the village midwife, and in between, you can keep up with your studies, read the latest journals. When we go up to London, you can do rounds with your Mrs. Crawford."

She lay back and looked up at him. He insisted on staying in her field of vision, so handsome and intense, his excitement infectious.

"Deliver babies? Make rounds? Your marchioness?"

"My marchioness."

His smile sent a shiver through her.

"You can help me craft bills to put forward. You can host fashionable soirees of like-minded people."

"Virgil, I am ruined. They will call me a..." She squeezed her eyes shut and thought of that day in the library. "A *whore*."

Compassion flared in his eyes, not pity, not anger either. "Did my brother use that word?"

She bit her lip and nodded.

"He was speaking from bitter experience, you know. He was poxed, and the cure didn't take."

"Oh." That was...startling. "Poor Caroline."

"I beg you, leave her out of our marriage bed. I haven't forgiven her yet for writing and pretending to be you."

"Why did she do it?"

"It was at his behest, I'd guess. He'd got rid of you, and he wanted to stop me from searching. Perhaps he didn't want us to be happy." He frowned down at her. "We can be happy, you know."

In his eyes she saw the same longing that infected her. She thought of his mother, kept away from her daughter by the father Ameline had rarely seen, and Virgil's brother, who in the end hadn't kept Virgil away from Ameline. And their girls. She thought of them.

Her heart filled and she reached for him. "Yes, yes, perhaps we can."

EPILOGUE

SNOW FELL ON THE DAY OF THEIR WEDDING, and Ameline bundled the girls up in heavy cloaks on top of their finery. All of Virgil's girls, his mother included, had new dresses, some of the stitches sewn by Longview girls who'd found employment in London. The girls were in pink, and Lady Wallenford in a forest green that matched her eyes. Ameline's gown was the finest she'd ever had, a blue that should make her feel worthy of this new life ahead.

Even wrapped in a cloak, she couldn't help the trembles besetting her, but she did try to hide them.

They'd all arrived at Willowbrook only a few days before. Virgil had insisted he'd marry his bride in the open for all to see, and Baker had arranged for the banns to be called in the local parish.

The whole village would turn out for a spectacle like this—the new lord they'd not seen for four years, and the bride whom he'd got with twins a few years before.

"Do look at this snow," Lady Wallenford said. Her smile was brave enough for both of them, but her lips trembled also.

Ameline reached for her hand and squeezed it. "I vow to not trip on my train, or bungle the wedding promises."

Lady Wallenford laughed. She'd been doing a lot of that lately, much more than Ameline had seen when she worked as Virgil's sister's companion.

Hackwell House had been filled with the same sort of laughter and, frankly, noise. She imagined the Hackwells were happy to send them packing. Except that, Lady Hackwell had deemed herself well enough to allow her husband to come with them and serve as best man.

Their other witness, Baker, was waiting at the church door to hand them down. Inside, Willowbrook maids took their cloaks and gave each girl a basket filled with the precious petals of greenhouse flowers.

Lady Wallenford smiled her reassurance and took charge of the girls. Ameline took Baker's arm and stepped into the vestibule.

The little church was packed to the rafters, and her skin rippled with the awareness of a hundred eyes following her.

Or—not her. Most of them glanced from the twins to Lady Wallenford and back again, smiling as the girls fumbled the petals and bumped into each other.

And then they noticed her. There was a collective indrawn breath.

"Steady then, my lady," Baker whispered.

My lady. She stood straighter. She would exit this church with a title, one that would give her burdens and cares she'd never wanted, and these people would look to Virgil and her, some for their livelihood, all of them for sound stewardship of the village and lands.

Baker had explained that to her when he'd shown her the household accounts. All the gazes swung to the front of the church, and Ameline's heart lifted.

At the altar stairs, Virgil greeted his daughters and mother. When he raised his eyes to her, she smiled and stepped out.

Hours later, they each carried a sleeping child to the nursery. The girls had come down to wish the last of the guests good night, and had fallen asleep on their father and grandmother's laps.

Ameline walked into the familiar room and waved off the dozing nursery maid. Virgil followed her through to the playroom and on into the bedchamber where they tucked the girls in and crept out.

She halted in the playroom. A table and chairs sat on one side, and a chest ran along the other, crammed with every sort of game and toy. There were books too. Virgil's sister had learned to read simple stories and liked books.

"Do you remember," she said, squeezing his hand.

He pulled her close. "Dulcie was laughing, and you were sitting there at that very table beaming at her, and I said to myself, that girl has the most delicious smile."

She laughed and went up on her toes and kissed him, and all the bitter memories became sweet again.

"I never once kissed you in the playroom, did I? Though I was sorely tempted that day."

"Nor in this bedroom," she whispered. "Though when Dulcie was dying, I wanted so for you to hold me." She sighed and stepped back. "Enough reminiscing. Come, before we shock the nursemaid."

"It's our wedding night."

"My point exactly," she said.

It was a miracle, this night. One she couldn't have seen coming when she arrived on Lady Hackwell's doorstep.

They tiptoed past the nursemaid, into the corridor, and down the stairs. "Of course," she said. "Most people would say we had our wedding night four years ago."

"And four weeks ago."

She laughed. "Well, given your great virility, my lord, perhaps we should discuss that business of recruiting a midwife for the village."

He opened the bedchamber door and clasped her to him, spending long moments exhibiting just how virile he could be.

And then he froze and set her back. "A midwife? Really?"

"It's far too soon to tell, but..."

"But you haven't cried off, not one night."

Virgil plopped down on the sofa and brought her down with him. "Good heavens." He laughed. "We might have as many as old George." He swiped a hand through his hair. "I'd best get to the books and find a way to make Willowbrook profitable."

"Yes," she said, untying his cravat, "but not tonight."

The End

If you enjoyed this book, please consider writing a review at any of the major book retailers, Amazon, Kobo, Barnes & Noble, iBooks, or at Goodreads.com.

A Note from the Author

Writing Ameline and Virgil's story took me deep into research of childbirth during the Regency period. If the subject interests you, information abounds on the internet. Especially helpful were articles by Anna Bosanquet, a Senior Lecturer in Midwifery at Kingston University/St. George's University of London.

I also delved in to the following books:

- *The King's Midwife, A History and Mystery of Madame du Coudray*, by Nina Rattner Gelbart
- *Smellie's Treatise on the Theory and Practice of Midwifery* (Available on Google Books)

Many thanks go to the generous authors of Romance Writers of America for advice and encouragement, with special thanks to author Alanna Lucas for insightful comments and moral support, and author and obstetrical nurse Suzanne Ferrell, who sat next to me at a book signing and let me pick her brain between chats with readers. Thanks also to Editor Tessa Shapcott for excellent advice and for lassoing my Americanisms, and to Cami Brite for the cover design.

And, as ever, I'm grateful to my husband for his unfailing support and enduring patience with dust bunnies and quick meals, and to my children who don't read romance, but still offer encouragement.

I love hearing from readers! You can contact and follow me on Facebook, Twitter, and Goodreads, and at my website AlinaKField.com. For special notices about sales and other news, please consider signing up for my newsletter at my website.

I promise I won't spam you or sell your email address!

Best regards, and happy reading!

Alina K. Field

Also by Alina K. Field

Bella's Band
A 2015 RONE Award Finalist
Soul Mate Publishing

A spinster's secrets tempt a killer—and steal a soldier's heart.

Bullets, blades, and incendiary bombs—Major Steven Beauverde, the latest Earl of Hackwell, belongs in *that* world, and is determined to get back to it. His brother's murder has forced Steven into a new and completely unwanted role, and worse, he has no idea how to salvage his family's depleted estate. A rumor that his brother had a son by a woman who may be a) the murderer, and b) his brother's secret wife, sets Steven on a mission to find her, the boy, and—Steven ardently hopes—the proof of a marriage that will set him free.

Confirmed spinster Annabelle Harris is a country heiress with a penchant for taking in orphans and helping the downtrodden. Her philanthropy hides her desperate search for her disgraced sister, the mistress to the Earl of Hackwell. When the Earl is murdered, her sister thrusts her child into Annabelle's care and disappears. Now, with suspicion pointing at the sister, Annabelle has begun a new quest, to find the woman, and clear her name.

When their paths converge, the reluctant Earl and the independent spinster find themselves rethinking their goals, and battling the real murderer together.

Available on Kindle from Amazon.

Rosalyn's Ring
2014 Book Buyer's Best Winner, Novella
Category
Soul Mate Publishing

A Christmas Wish Becomes a Christmas Miracle

With her true inheritance lost, Rosalyn Montagu has reluctantly fallen into her elderly cousin's tidy London life of do-gooder spinster. But when a young woman from the district of Rosalyn's childhood is put up for auction in a wife sale, Rosalyn seizes the chance to rescue her—and to recover a treasured family heirloom, her father's signet ring.

Intent on liberating the young wife, Rosalyn braves a precarious Christmas Eve coach ride in the company of a mysterious nobleman and soon finds she's not the only determined buyer attending the sale. Her rakish opponent not only thwarts her purchase, he reveals himself as the man who took everything that should have been hers—everything but her father's ring, which she recovers before being tossed out of the inn into the snowy night.

The newly anointed Viscount Cathmore has surrendered to his father's dream of accession to a social class he disdains, but he's drawn the line at marrying a blue-blooded miss. Then he meets Rosalyn, a provoking beauty with an upper crust manner, a larcenous streak, and enough secrets to rouse even his jaded heart, including the truth of her identity. But more mysteries swirl around Rosalyn's lost inheritance, and Cathmore is just the man to help her uncover the truth.

Available on Kindle from Amazon.

Liliana's Letter
Finalist, 2015 National Reader's Choice
Award
Havenlock Press

The Matchmaker Meets the Matchbreaker

The Matchmaker

Lord Grigsby wants nothing more than to retreat to his study, but a promise to his long-dead sister has forced him back into society to broker the marriage of his nephew to the heiress whose money can save the young man's earldom. If only the young lady's starchy hired companion would move out of the way.

The Matchbreaker

Hired to launch an heiress's society debut, seemingly straitlaced spinster Liliana Ashford's future as a professional chaperone depends on the girl's successful marriage. But Liliana had her own close encounter with a scoundrel years ago, and she won't let her charge be forced into marriage to the same kind of rogue, no matter how hard the man's widowed uncle tries to woo Liliana around to the match.

Secrets and a Scandalous Murder

A shadow from Liliana's past appears bearing an unfortunate letter she wrote long ago, and then the earl is murdered, evoking the scandal of the season. While she scrambles to make a respectable match for her charge before her own past can be exposed, Grigsby sets about finding his nephew's killer—and Liliana's secrets.

Available in paperbook from Amazon, and as an ebook from Amazon, Kobo, Barnes & Noble, iBooks, and GooglePlay Books

Coming in 2017

The Bastard's Iberian Bride, the first book in a new Regency series from Alina K. Field.

Find out more at AlinaKField.com!

43783795R00099

Made in the USA
San Bernardino, CA
27 December 2016